Praise for *She Who Knows, A Tale of the Heart*

"A heart touching and inspiring story of a young woman's drive to overcome obstacles and learn to love. Set in a different place and era, with a touch of Hawaiian folklore, readers will root for Cassandra to grow into the woman she longs to be."

Jane Ameel,
former Director, Waukesha,
Wisconsin, Public Library

"Barbara Bras has a refreshing style that is easy and effortless. Her expressions and details are what writers long for and readers hope to absorb."

Linda Barnett-Johnson,
Professional Virtual Assistant for Authors

"She Who Knows, A Tale of the Heart tells the compelling story of Cassandra Bras's fascinating tale captures the inner struggles of her character with imagination and sensitivity, and in the lush tropical setting, you'll find yourself rooting for Cassie to find her way through her life's hardships until the tender, satisfying conclusion. An unforgettable read!"

Kim Kendall
http://kimkendallauthor.com

"This delightful story captivated my attention and kept me reading to the end of the book. Cassandra is a real and engaging character, and the conflicts that she faces throughout the story had me turning the pages to discover how things were resolved. I loved the Hawaiian setting in this story and her use of the Menehunes and their gift added an interesting twist. I highly recommend this book."

Holly E. Messick,
Author and retired Librarian

"Reminiscent of Dickens, **She Who Knows, A Tale of the Heart,** is a warm, engaging, delightful story that will change your heart as well. Well-written with a touching story line and vivid imagery, author Barbara Bras has created a jewel of a book."

Lori A. Moore,
Award-Winning Author

"I loved this story and breezed straight through it. It serves as a well-written reminder to honor the present and never take for granted the life and love you are given."

Kylie Crawford TenBrook, attorney

"Bras gives wings to your soul and flight to your heart in her delightful and heartwarming tale about Cassie. Set within a lush and sometimes magical Hawaiian landscape, the story will invoke a sense of youth's blossoming and emergence from isolation. Though

Cassie believes the mystical Menehune's Gift is what makes her powerful, she discovers, similar to *The Wonderful Wizard of Oz*'s Dorothy, that real magic is within, as she unearths pathways to heal her heart. You will instantly embrace *She Who Knows: A Tale from the Heart* as a new classic for your collection."

Elizabeth Onyeabor, Author and Poet,
http://elizabethonyeabor.com

"This is a sweet story of growing up unloved and alone – and finding both love and "family" after years of searching."

Bill Worth,
novelist and editor

She Who Knows

A Tale of the Heart

Barbara Bras

Barbara Bras Books are available for order through Ingram Press Catalogues

Barbara Bras

Visit my website at www.AuthorBBras.com

Printed in the United States of America

First Printing: May 2016

Published by Sojourn Publishing, LLC

ISBN: 978-1-62747-214-2
Ebook ISBN: 978-1-62747-215-9

Dedication

In memory of Barbara Robinson, who first told me her story while teaching at Roosevelt High School in Honolulu, Hawaii.

Prologue

The little girl held her father's hand tightly as they boarded the ship for Maui. No pleasure ships had operated between the islands since Pearl Harbor. The vessel held supplies and a few business people. In 1945, a little girl properly dressed for travel wore a dress and pinafore, with hair perfectly curled into long dark ropes and a large pink bow fastened on top.

She knew her mother was gone. Suddenly sick and then gone forever. Cassandra couldn't remember much about her even now except that she would call her over; drawing her so close that Cassandra could smell her rosewater.

"Keep your eyes and ears open – you never know what you are going to see." Other times she would hold Cassandra tightly and whisper into her ear, "My dear girl, my dear Cassandra, think well of your mother, and help your father. Remember, nothing is ever what it appears to be." None of it made much sense to five-year-old Cassandra, but her mother's sweet smell lingered in her mind and she repeated her words often so that she would never forget. Even now as she thought of it, she swallowed a small sob.

The day her mother died, she stood in the dining room and watched silently as they took her still body out the front door. She didn't cry, she simply observed it as if in a dream. Afterward, her father walked toward her, knelt down and looked into her face, right into her eyes. She stepped away from him; seeing him so close frightened her. She saw no hint of softness, only his somber serious look, the large dark beard and those black eyes boring into hers. "Cassandra, your mother is gone now and I am afraid the timing couldn't be worse. You know what the doctors said at Children's Hospital, we have to do something quickly or you will never get better." His stern voice didn't invite a response, but Cassandra nodded her head the tiniest bit anyway. Yes, she remembered. "Cassandra, listen to me. I must send you away, to your grandparents' home on Maui, where I grew up. When you recover, you can return home to Oahu. Do you understand?" He didn't wait for her to answer; instead, he rose, turned and left the room. She stood there.

No, she didn't understand at all, except that he wouldn't be with her and he would leave her in Maui, alone. The next day her father accompanied her to the ship. This time he didn't look her in the eyes, instead he towered over her, staring out at the ocean. "You must understand Cassandra; being in the mountain air will help you get better. You won't be completely alone. Your nurse will be with you and Mr. and Mrs. Morimoto have lived there since I was a child. I cannot stay with you because I have my law practice to attend to." Then, almost as an afterthought, he added, "But I will come see you as often as I can."

She knew she shouldn't cry and make him angry, but the hot tears escaping down her cheeks had a mind of their own. No more mother and her father would leave her in a strange place. Adopting her father's austere manner, she stood up as tall as she could, wiped the tears from her cheeks and stoically looked forward.

1

Maui, 1950

As the sun kissed her face, Cassandra opened her eyes. She looked out the window from her room at the top of the three-story house and saw the green of the sugarcane fields and beyond to the bluest sky offset by the ocean's differing shade. Cassandra still had her long brown hair but she mostly wore it up in a ponytail. She liked to brush it herself and frequently begged Nurse to leave her alone so that she could do just that. She took it down only at night when she went to bed.

She had a book about Helen Keller with pictures of her as a young girl and Cassandra would study them and then look at herself in the mirror. Hers wasn't as lovely, she decided, just the empty face of a dark-haired girl who might be prettier if she smiled more often.

Alone as usual to welcome the new day, she heard Nurse downstairs noisily preparing her breakfast and medications. Her father, along with Dr. Fellows, would arrive in a week for her monthly examination. She felt well, but after every exam the doctor simply shook his head and said, "Not yet, my dear girl, not yet."

However, she knew different, she could feel her heart, stronger and healthier. She spent most days reading, but for whole days recently, she didn't feel like reading at all. Last week Nurse said, "Why don't you write? At least begin a diary or journal. Think what you can imagine while sitting up here looking out at the ocean." To reinforce her idea, Nurse now placed new sharp pencils and pages of cream lined writing paper in front of her.

"My letters aren't very good yet," she said, and stared blankly at the new materials.

Nurse glared at her, "But you practice them all the time, surely you must be better by now. Show me." Cassandra slowly made the marks on the writing paper as Nurse watched and then shook her head. "Such poor letters for a ten-year-old. Clearly, you need more practice. Now is a good time, begin immediately."

Cassandra practiced her letters for a while after Nurse left, but soon she dropped her pencil and stared out at the ocean. She wasn't exactly certain when she became dissatisfied with life in her room, but she suspected it was when she began reading books about girls who had friends and even sisters. Dr. Fellows had brought her a copy of *Little Women* for her birthday and she knew from page one that she had never read such a story. In fact, nothing she had read came close to describing the joys of sisterhood and friendship.

This new knowledge awakened in her a deep longing she hadn't known existed. She imagined it was not unlike Adam and Eve in the garden when they knew that they were naked. She now knew she was truly alone. It also occurred to her that all along she had hoped every visit the doctor and her father made to Maui would be the one when they declared her well enough to return home to Oahu. She imagined attending school with other children, playing games or singing

2

silly songs. If she ever spent time with other children, she didn't remember it.

Her only memory outside of this house consisted of the journey up the mountainside from Kahului. She thought she remembered the little cart and horse that carried her to this house, until she saw an old picture of the cart. A smaller version of herself, dressed for traveling, sat next to her father. Perhaps the picture provided the memory, her last memory of anywhere except this room and this house, now her prison. It was not surprising that her memories were few, having barely turned five years old when she arrived in Maui. Every year thereafter on her birthday, her father would send a special little cake even though Nurse never allowed her to eat it. She remembered the cake and crying on her birthday. Strangely enough, she didn't remember being ill, unless she counted the times she fainted and Nurse would force her to stay in bed and lie quietly for unbearably dull, long days.

Now that she could read, her boredom lessened, but new books rarely arrived. Her father tried to remember one for her when he visited. One of her first books was Robert Louis Stevenson's *A Child's Garden of Verse,* which she liked so much that her tutor, Mr. Hunter, lent her a small volume about the author. Once she learned that he, too, was an only child and quite sickly she felt an immediate closeness to him. Soon after he had lent her the book, she overheard a conversation between Mr. Hunter and Nurse from which she surmised that they both thought her a bit odd like Mr. Stevenson, and that like him she had spent too much time with her books and not enough with other children.

She enjoyed Robert Louis Stevenson's tales of sea captains because they reminded her of her grandfather, also a seafaring man. On one of his first voyages as Captain to the Hawaiian Islands, he hosted a group of musicians who were traveling there to perform and then enjoy a holiday. Her grandmother, a violinist studying to be a professor of music in San Francisco, caught the Captain's eye, according to her father. Her life changed when she met the Captain. She played the violin for the rest of her life, but she never returned to San Francisco to study or for anything else.

Cassandra loved the story of her grandfather and grandmother and although she spent the first five years of her life on Oahu, her grandparents had always lived on Maui. Their home, a picture of Victorian grandeur, sat on a strange and remote spot high above the ocean. Because the Captain demanded to see the ocean at all times, every part of the house boasted large windows to accommodate his wishes. The idea of living in their house, even though she never knew them, somehow pleased her. She spent hours looking at their pictures and imagining her father growing up there. Her father said that the Captain, a stern man, refused to tell tales of his life at sea, but his mother, a great storyteller, shared many stories of the Menehune, the little people of Hawaii. Once or twice as a child, her father sat with her and as if talking to himself, repeated his mother's stories. Cassandra pictured her father in the house, sitting and listening to his mother. She imagined his loneliness as similar to hers, up in the mountains with no other children to play with. It was that thought alone that made her father seem real to her.

Although her grandparents had died long ago, photographs of those days littered the large house. Pictures of her grandparents newly married and of her father as a child, framed in heavy ornate wood, adorned every room except hers. All featured unsmiling figures dressed for special occasions and formally posed, the custom in the early part of the century. One picture differed; it was a snapshot of her parents smiling broadly at one another. She decided pictures weren't as good as seeing a person in real life. Cassandra sighed; thinking of the pictures reminded her of her solitude, and her conscience reminded her of her incomplete schoolwork. She decided to concentrate on the work in front of her, but then decided that if she closed her eyes for a minute it would help her focus.

Almost immediately, her nose alerted her to the nearness of plants, like those she knew from her grandparents' garden. Ah, just a dream she thought, before she even opened her eyes. As she did, she thought she recognized the place, a clearing in a valley with enormous stalks of bamboo on one side and towering tropical palms and ferns on the other. She heard a rustling noise coming from the bamboo on her left, and she turned, expecting to see a horse or other small animal. Then she saw him. She looked closer in the dim light. A very old man, quite tiny, perhaps only three feet tall. He saw her too, gave her a wink and a smile, and then ran off into the woods.

"Wait, please wait. I wish to talk to you." Cassandra ran into the woods after him, but soon the dim light vanished and she couldn't see anything. Shaking and a bit scared she tried to look around. If this is a dream she wondered, why do I feel like I have been here before; why is everything so familiar? She inched her way forward, waiting for her eyes to adjust in the dark. What she saw made her heart race and her stomach flip, but as the truth dawned on her she was no longer afraid. Yes, she had seen the Menehune that she had heard of and recently read about in a book Dr. Fellows had brought her.

She had learned that according to Hawaiian legend, before the first settlers arrived from Polynesia, the Menehune inhabited the islands. They were a mischievous group of small people who lived hidden in the forests and valleys and roamed the deep forests at night. They were reported to be about two feet tall, though some were as tiny as six inches, small enough to fit in the palm of a hand.

As she marveled at this, her excitement grew – then it is true, they do exist. She heard a little giggle behind her and turned again, now surprised to see a little woman. She was dressed in a single banana leaf with a sparkling butterfly in her curly black hair, her bronzed skin glowing. Studying Cassandra closely, she smiled, held up her tiny hand and motioned her to follow. Cassandra obeyed as if in a trance, holding her breath, unsure of what it all meant. As she carefully followed, the tropical forest grew even darker, and the air became still and tomblike. She could smell the moist leaves below her feet and no longer heard birds or any noise other than her own soft footsteps. She stumbled, lost her footing and tripped, and when she stood up, she no longer saw the tiny woman. She groped around in the darkness. "Help. Come back, please, I don't know the way out." Her voice sounded strange and choked and tears now wet her face. Out of the stillness she heard a voice say, "Remember, the little people aren't dangerous, they're only a bit mischievous."

She called again, "Hey there, please come back. I promise I won't hurt you." A bronze light began to form a ring around her. Then she saw them, so many she couldn't believe it. The light made it difficult to distinguish the men from women. Then out of the dim glow, a child with matted hair and dark skin timidly stepped toward her, hands lightly clasped as if keeping an insect trapped inside. None of them spoke as they encircled Cassandra, crowding in closer and closer. As they came nearer she stammered, "Uh, what is it? A praying mantis or a walking stick? Come now; let me see what you have in your hands." She felt impatience growing and she longed to reach out and snatch it out of the child's hands.

The child slowly opened her hands and the tiniest dragonfly, no more than a thimble big, sat in her palm. As Cassandra watched, frozen in amazement, the little dragonfly opened its wings as if to fly and revealed it was no such creature at all. Cassandra bent down to examine it closely. There lay a miniature dragon with sparkling green wings, deep purple-blue eyes, and a crest of gold. She watched transfixed as it fluttered up and down again. It looked at Cassandra, its head cocked to one side, as if it had a question for her.

Cassandra held out her hand, which seemed like the thing to do. Suddenly the dragon flew to her hand and settled down almost as if it wanted to sleep. Someone next to Cassandra said something to the child in a language that sounded familiar, but she couldn't decipher it. It sounded like someone sped up a record, but very softly. As the others nodded, the child walked over to Cassandra, covered the little thing with her hands, and when she removed them, the dragon was gone.

At the same time, Cassandra felt the oddest fluttering inside of her, right inside her tummy. She looked around, looking frantically for a sign of the little dragon. It occurred to her that she had swallowed it, and with that thought, she began to panic. This dream felt too real and difficult to comprehend.

"Cassandra? Cassandra?" From down below Nurse's booming voice called her awake. "You should be working on your homework, not napping. Mr. Hunter will be here soon, what will you show for yourself?"

2

U h oh. Cassandra's eyes flew open. She jumped up from her bed and searched her desk for the incomplete schoolwork. Rather than finish her grammar worksheets and math problems, she had spent much of the past week daydreaming about attending a real school with other children. She imagined they were dear and friendly, helping each other with lessons and looking out for one another. She wished for a friend of her own to share secrets with. These visions consumed her thoughts and kept her from her schoolwork.

Mr. Hunter, she reminded herself. Sighing, she stared miserably at her math problems, hoping magically to calculate at least a few before his arrival. He wouldn't be cross with her, but she hated the thought of disappointing him. His visits marked a bright spot in her dull existence and she adored earning his smiles. He arrived in the islands newly graduated from seminary and expected to form his own congregation, but the church fathers viewed unmarried young ministers as unprepared for such a task. Instead, Mr. Hunter assumed the role of parish teacher. He taught the small grade school in Kahului and each week struggled up the steep road to oversee her lessons. He smelled of the sandalwood that Mrs. Morimoto, the housekeeper, burned at times. Taller than her father, his carefully combed golden-brown hair allowed one renegade strand to escape and stand at attention on the crown of his head. Overall, he left the impression of a boy rather than a man.

Serious and stern while Nurse hovered, once alone with her, he amused her with funny stories about village life and the children's antics in his classroom. The children of missionaries and other church workers, many of his pupils possessed proper biblical names. Eventually she felt as if she knew Ruth, Sarah, Matthew, Mark and Peter. Her face lit up as she heard his voice downstairs. She waited expectantly as she heard him begin the many steps to her landing.

"Hello, Cassandra." Mr. Hunter paused, breathless like most who made the steep climb to the room at the top of the house. "How are you on this glorious day that our Lord has made?" He dressed, as always, in traditional European fashion with a herringbone wool vest, heavy pants and a long grey cutaway coat. In spite of the cooler temperatures on her mountaintop, his costume and the climb birthed beads of sweat on his forehead and upper lip. He positioned himself in the floral overstuffed armchair across from Cassandra's desk, and used a handkerchief to wipe his face. He bestowed one of his endearing smiles upon her.

Her shame prompted her to begin. "Oh Mr. Hunter. I truly am very sorry to report to you the truth about these lessons." She paused and then looked down into her lap.

He said simply, "Oh?" But he thought to himself, *Now what story is this little moppet going to tell me today about why her lessons aren't finished?*

"What. . . whatever do you mean?" Cassandra stammered as she looked up at him, surprised at his language and tone.

"I simply said 'Oh' Cassandra, because I wondered what prevented you from doing your lessons all week. Surely I didn't assign you that much work and I know you don't have much else to keep you occupied." He stopped speaking but his thought continued, *What am I going to do with her? This will never do. Her father will be angry with me and he will surely remove me from my position as her tutor.*

Cassandra stared at him as she heard the last two statements. No doubt, she heard his voice say the words, but she could see that his lips never moved. Curious, she cautiously formed the words and ventured, "And why do you think my father will remove you as my tutor Mr. Hunter?"

His face registered shock and surprise. He leaned over, peered at her and said, "Pardon me, but what did you say?"

She carefully repeated, "Why did you say you thought my father would terminate you?"

"I, I didn't." He stammered, as his cheeks turned a bright red. "In fact, I am sure I said no such thing. Now let's get to your lessons and stop this nonsense."

For the rest of the hour Cassandra didn't hear anything else, but she watched his lips closely and finally as he stood to leave she heard clearly, *Now before our next lesson* and she realized she had heard a thought because he didn't speak. He finished it aloud, "Now before our next lesson I expect you will complete every one of your assignments. No excuses next time." Shocked and confused at his severe tone, she offered nothing in response. Mr. Hunter, who had never spoken harshly to her, abruptly left the room.

She lay on her bed, her mind a jumble of thoughts. Did I imagine it, or did he actually think those things? Did he say the words aloud, but I simply failed to see his lips move? Left to herself for the rest of the afternoon, she picked up her notebook and began to write. Until now, she wrote dull stories, nothing more than copies of those read to her as a child or those she read in her books. How exciting to finally have something interesting to write about. Lest she forget about her dream, she grabbed a pencil and began to write quickly, now unhindered by any difficulty forming the letters. The description of woods, the strange darkness, the sudden appearance of the Menehune and their silence all appeared magically on the page before her. As she reached the part about the dragon's disappearance, she worried that the little dragon could be inside her. She lay flat on the bed and felt her stomach. She poked and prodded but felt nothing, except a little rumble because she had skipped her mid-day meal and forgot to ask Nurse for tea during Mr. Hunter's lessons. She could see the sun setting out her window. Nurse would bring dinner soon. She decided to watch her carefully to see if she could hear anything unusual.

Soon she heard Nurse lumbering up the stairs with her supper tray. She called her Nurse ever since she could remember, and never considered asking her name. The fact that her name described her job struck her as strange now. For some reason, Nurse dressed as she would in a hospital, in a crisp white uniform, although without a nurse's cap. She smelled of antiseptic or cleaning fluid; a smell that Cassandra associated with her alone. A broad-shouldered, stocky woman of an uncertain age, she took her time coming up the stairs. Slowly, her heavy shoes on the teak wood stairs creaked with her weight. Cassandra watched as she entered and heard plainly: *I do hope this girl eats her dinner tonight. Her heart is never going to heal if she doesn't eat properly.* Nurse's lips never moved. Cassandra's mouth fell open and immediately Nurse ordered, "Young lady. Close that mouth this instant. Manners." Then she turned her back to Cassandra as she set about fixing her dinner tray and medications.

"Uh, Nurse?" She began slowly, mentally formulating her question. Nurse swung around "Yes, what is it?"

"Nurse, do you think it is possible for one person to know what another person is thinking or know what they are going to say before they say it?"

"Preposterous." Nurse practically snorted the words in response. "You are spending too much time reading those silly books instead of getting a proper education." Then she continued, "Tell me where you got such a silly idea. Not from Mr. Hunter I trust."

"Oh well, kind of," she lied. Then she decided on another approach. "Nurse, do you think if I eat all of this my heart will get better?" It was Nurse's turn to close her mouth, now fallen open in surprise.

"Listen Miss Cassandra, I said no such thing. Why on earth would you say that?" Privately Nurse wondered, *Who would have told her about her heart?*

In fact, due to Cassandra's age and lack of exposure to the outside world, the doctors decided it best if she knew nothing of her condition. They believed that relocating to the mountains would allow the thin, dry mountain air and bedrest to heal the hole in her heart. It was a common treatment for a heart defect in 1945.

Cassandra began to understand that for whatever reason she heard people's thoughts, and heard them quite clearly when they thought to themselves without speaking at the same time. How complicated, she thought, I wonder if I can also distinguish what people will say even before they say it.

Nurse's contorted face opposite her reminded her that she owed her an answer. "Sorry, Nurse, never mind then, I guess it was just something I thought about. Please, I am not hungry at all, only very tired. I think I will go to sleep now." She pushed the tray away and gave Nurse a weak smile. Nurse glared at her, silently took the tray and went back the way she came, clumping down the stairs.

3

Nurse probably knew she had lied, but Cassandra needed time alone to think. This new information required testing in order to comprehend its potential, its power. For the first time, Cassandra allowed herself to wonder if the gift of the little dragon could help her get the one thing she wanted, a life with other children. She fell fast asleep while devising her plans.

Over the next few days, Cassandra learned what she could about her new Gift, which is how she now thought of it. Her regular heart doctor, Dr. Fellows, would travel with her father to the island to see her. Examination day's special privileges included her father carrying her downstairs, a walk in the garden after the examination and dinner in the dining room. She felt the excitement of her plan bubbling up inside of her; she couldn't wait for them to arrive. In the past, she played the obedient little girl, a girl perfect for the times, not asking questions, and not causing any trouble. Her father's stern demeanor and formal tone generally made her anxious about his visits, but today she felt something quite different. The Gift had opened her mind so that she could now hear thoughts. It would show her the truth and she planned to use it to leave her grandparents' home and go to school in Oahu.

Her father appeared at the landing, slightly winded. "Cassandra. Are you ready for Doctor Fellow's examination?"

"Yes, Father, I am." She swung her legs over the bed and reached out for him to pick her up. His muscular arms scooped her up easily and she wrapped her thin arms around his neck, the only time she ever touched him. She inhaled the spice he wore, reminding her of cloves combined with something else she couldn't identify, but always associated with her father. Quickly they descended the three flights of stairs to the entryway and then into the large front parlor. She noticed that she hadn't heard any thoughts from her father. As he placed her on the chair she asked, "Father?"

"Yes, Cassandra?"

"May I ask you a question?" Suddenly she heard him wonder, *What is this strange behavior? She usually doesn't ask questions. I wonder if Mr. Hunter has been putting strange thoughts in her head, as Nurse told me.*

"Father, I know I usually don't ask questions, but today I have one. When may I come back to Oahu? I truly wish to attend a real school where I might have playmates or friends." She heard her father's thought, *Is that all she wants out of life? Merely the chance to play with some friends? My goodness I can think of a thousand things that are more important.* But aloud he said, "It's too dangerous for you, Cassandra. I thought you understood that you can't run or play like the other children yet. Perhaps in a year or two." Then he thought, *Well, perhaps the child has a point. Now that she is older and could mind herself, perhaps she could experiment with attending a school here on Maui.*

Cassandra jumped up and clapped her hands. "Oh, could I father, could I?" She was so excited at hearing his thought that she failed to see the surprised and angry look on his face.

"What in God's name are you talking about Cassandra? Could you what?"

"Oh, sorry Father. Forgive me. For a moment, I thought you said I might go to school here on Maui. I would be very careful and not run or get into any trouble, I promise."

The doctor's entrance interrupted her father. Clearly shocked by Cassandra's appearance, he called her to him.

"Come here my dear girl. What has gotten into you, I wonder? Your cheeks are bright red and you look overexcited. Yes, you are warm. Tell me what has happened to cause this kind of reaction in my favorite patient."

"Oh, Dr. Fellows, Father and I were discussing whether I might attend school here on Maui." Then she quickly added, "Of course, that is unless I am well enough to return home." She smiled her best smile in the doctor's direction. Dr. Fellows thought *The poor little thing. I would guess she is quite lonely stuck up in that room with no playmates and only her books to read.*

Her father interrupted the doctor's thought. "And John, to be very clear about this I have no idea where she got that notion, as I have not said one word about it. I intend to find out who could have put such an idea in her head." As the two men continued their conversation, the

17

Gift's working became clearer to Cassandra. She found that she could distinguish when a person was thinking from when they were speaking without staring at their lips. Thoughts sounded more like loud whispers than spoken words. She also noticed she couldn't hear her father's thoughts when she focused on the doctor's thoughts. A bit complicated, but she practiced by forcing herself to look at the forehead of the person whose thoughts she wished to hear.

Concerned that his patient looked overwrought, Dr. Fellows sat down on the large sofa and took control. "Come over here Cassandra and let me take a look at you." As she complied, he pulled out his stethoscope and began the long routine of listening to her heart over and over again, asking her to breathe in and out and so on. She knew the routine well after five years and didn't require any prompting.

Sighing, she turned to him. "Well, Dr. Fellows? What do you think? Am I better? Can I go to school here in Maui?" She heard Dr. Fellows, *Where is all this coming from? She has always been content to entertain herself with her books and maps and never once mentioned leaving. I seriously hope this seclusion hasn't created negative behavioral side effects.*

Cassandra listened carefully and began to execute her plan. "Mr. Hunter said it would be good for me to conduct my studies with other children; that I might benefit from exposure to them." Her father and the doctor stared at her.

"He said that, did he?" her father asked.

"Well yes, in so many words, his concern is that it is difficult for me to concentrate on my studies without other children around to help me."

Her father thought, *Why is Mr. Hunter interfering by telling the child this? If he felt that way, why wouldn't he tell me?* He said, "Never mind that now, it is time for your walk in the garden. Would you have me call Nurse to take you or are you all right alone? I wish to speak with the doctor for a few minutes. When you finish you may return to the parlor."

"Please allow me a walk by myself, Father. After spending weeks upstairs, I wish to take my time on this beautiful day appreciating my Grandparents' garden." Seeing her father's nod as he turned to the doctor, she quickly walked out of the parlor, glad that her shaky legs held her up.

4

To avoid Nurse, Cassandra exited the house through the dining room French doors. Her grandparents brought many plants from the United States and England and peppered them alongside the native Hawaiian specimens to create their garden. Her grandmother sketched the native plants and submitted them to botanical journals on the mainland. Many of her sketches now graced the walls of the dining room. Cassandra paused for a moment in front of one entitled *The Hāpuʻu*, a tree fern she had yet to discover in the garden. She studied it closely, noting the frond's intricate design and the size of the stem. Searching for the plants amused her and brought her closer to the garden's creators, now long gone. Mrs. Morimoto, the family's cook and housekeeper, who lived in the house for more than fifty years, told Cassandra that at one time her grandmother had small porcelain signs identifying the various species for visitors to the garden. Today no signs existed, but she didn't mind, as she enjoyed the challenge of matching each plant to its drawing.

As she wandered the little footpaths, hearing the songs of the birds and relishing the moist garden air on her skin, she wondered what her grandmother thought as she worked in the garden. Did she imagine that someday her own granddaughter would live here or, as Cassandra thought, live as a prisoner here? The questions returned now; what happened to her, why could she suddenly hear people's thoughts? Was her mind playing tricks on her? In the past, she experienced a fleeting sensation that she knew a place or that an event happened before, but nothing like this. Whenever she chose, she would look toward the person, focus and hear their thoughts. Their secret, private thoughts.

As she reached the center of the garden, she paused in front of the towering banyan tree. Surrounded by the garden, no one could see her from the house. As a small child, she thought of the banyan's long trunks as arms that reached out to her. She imagined that the enormous tree with its protrusions was a kind, elderly grandmother inviting her to be gently rocked to sleep. She did what she did as a child, settling herself on the soft mat between the huge protruding roots. She closed her eyes and felt herself sinking into the mossy ground beneath her.

She saw the girl Menehune giving her the little dragon and it reminded her of something and she opened her eyes, alarmed. Oh no. Mrs. Morimoto told her that long ago, the Menehune would put a spell on a person and eventually that person would become one of them. To the outside world, it appeared that the person had died, but instead they magically became a little person, forever happy to live in the valleys and the waterfalls of the islands. Although they required neither food nor drink, sometimes for fun they took things from the families' homes. Whenever she lost a special dish or utensil, Mrs. Morimoto would exclaim, "See? Ha, the Menehune was here."

Cassandra observed the numerous leaves above her, squinting to see the sky through the thick, glossy foliage. It occurred to her that the Menehune's spell rested upon her now and death would come next. She took stock of what she knew: she saw the Menehune; she held the dragon, which now lived inside of her, and the doctor pronounced her heart no worse, but no better. Her conclusion; she would die and become an invisible little person, a Menehune. Tears came to her eyes. To stop them, she closed her eyes tightly, not wanting to see anything else, but she did; a light, a blue-green light the color of the ocean she could see from her window. Typically unafraid of the dark night or the huge storms that would come in from the sea; now deep inside of her she felt fear. Lying there with her eyes closed she examined it. What exactly she wondered, do I fear? Could it be dying? It had never occurred to her that she might die. Only old people died, like Mr. Greeley who used to bring groceries to the house. She had asked Mr. Morimoto why he had died and he said, "It time, it time to die, no big deal. He old, it time, you young, not time for you, no worry."

She sighed and slowly disentangled herself from the banyan roots and made her way back to the house. An idea bubbled up in her mind. Instead of reading thoughts or knowing what someone might say before they said it, she wondered if she could use The Gift to make someone do whatever she wanted, and that would certainly be useful. She remembered a story about a man who could do that simply by concentrating very hard on his victim's thoughts. As simple as planting a seed, he said.

It seemed reasonable to her that she might use The Gift the same way. She opened the kitchen door and walked past Mrs. Morimoto, so immersed in her dinner preparations she didn't bother to look up. When her father visited, he allowed Cassandra to join them for the evening meal on the condition that she retire to bed immediately afterwards. Usually she dreaded the meal because her father rarely spoke directly to her or allowed her to engage in the conversation. Now she could see an excellent opportunity for her to conduct an experiment.

5

"Cassandra? Is that you? Come into the parlor," her father called. She entered and found both men looking stern and solemn in their upright chairs with their teacups beside them. Her father began, "We discussed your condition at length, Cassandra, and we believe the time has come to share the entire story with you. I must admit, I have thought of you as a little child until today when the good Doctor here convinced me of your ability to comprehend the truth. Sit down and allow me to begin, and please do not interrupt."

Surprised at his frank statement, Cassandra dropped onto the ottoman directly in front of him and waited for him to begin. The parlor furniture hailed from another era, remnants of the Captain's original set shipped from the mainland, now faded and slightly worn. Cassandra's seat was her favorite, an ottoman the size of an armchair, covered in a deep royal purple velvet. She focused on her father and heard, *I certainly hope I am making the right decision; I don't want any kind of emotional reaction.* She couldn't help it; she nodded in agreement and then caught herself. She volunteered, "Please continue Father, I am old enough to understand."

"All right Cassandra. At birth, the doctor pronounced you a perfectly healthy little girl, and although you possessed a healthy appetite, you didn't grow as expected. Then when you turned, what age, John?"

The doctor said, "I believe soon after her fourth birthday."

"Oh yes, that's right, that's when you began exhibiting what the doctors could only describe as fainting spells. I recall once at dinner you fell right out of your chair, and another time while walking with your mother you collapsed on the ground. Naturally, these incidents caused us a great deal of worry. Although you usually woke right up, you didn't seem, how should I explain it, you didn't seem right. Yes, that's it, not yourself for a little while. We thought it might be as simple as overexertion. We took you to various doctors in Honolulu, and they examined you, admitted you to the hospital and eventually X-rayed your heart." He sighed at the memory. "It revealed a larger than average size hole in your heart. At first, the doctors didn't recommend surgery and thought that with the right treatment it would close by itself. They proposed spending a significant amount of time in the higher elevations of Maui with its clean mountain air, complete bedrest and no exposure to other children. At the very least, they believed that with this course of action you would have a chance to become stronger. I delayed bringing you to Maui only due to your mother's illness, which occurred soon after your release from the hospital."

She stared at him, waiting to hear if he had more to say. Finally he said, "You look like you have seen a ghost, are you all right Cassandra?" All thoughts of her experiment had left her and now she considered whether to tell him about the many times she had dreamt of the hospital.

In her dreams, she woke alone in the dimly lit hospital room to hear adult voices, but none that she recognized. She looked around, but couldn't see anyone nearby. She got up from the hospital bed and walked out into the hall, looking for them. Although she couldn't make out what they were saying, she definitely heard talking. As she walked past the other patients' rooms, she saw that they were all the same, empty. Nearing the source of the voices, she began to distinguish their words, "She won't live to be six years old at this rate, the sea air is too harsh for her lungs and she has already had too many fainting spells."

Another voice said, "Yes, I fear her brain may be damaged as well. She needs to be moved soon."

Yet another man's voice said, "Her parents expect a prognosis. I for one don't know what to tell them. Perhaps she will get better with this treatment, but who knows?"

The voice of the first man said, "If she gets any one of the island fevers I don't think her heart will survive, even with a drier climate and bed rest." At this point, she would wake up, and now her father's words confirmed what she already knew.

"Cassandra. I asked if you were alright." Her father looked intently at her, impatiently waiting for her response.

"Yes, yes, I am fine." Unsure how to proceed she added, "Thank you for explaining this to me. It may surprise you Father, but I often dreamed that I heard the doctors discussing my heart and sending me away. Perhaps I heard something while in the hospital, but in any event, I already thought this to be true."

She saw her father exchange a look with Dr. Fellows and then he said, "I am afraid you missed the entire point of my explanation. I had hoped you would grasp the reasons why you are here and why for the time being you must remain here."

Cassandra knelt down in front of her father. "But Father, after five years I believe the doctors would consider a new treatment for me. Please, I know my own heart and I know its strength. I will soon celebrate 11 years. Please don't make me stay here any longer. May I return to Oahu with you and attend regular school?"

Her father, shocked at her outburst thought, *What should I make of this strange behavior? Perhaps the doctor is correct in that this solitude is more harmful than helpful for the child.* Instead, he firmly stated, "That is enough. We will see after the doctor's next visit. Please go wash for dinner and tell Mrs. Morimoto we are ready."

Later that evening as she reflected on the day, she thought how little hearing other's thoughts helped her during that conversation. Her father's reaction didn't surprise her, as he hated any display of emotion, but she had surprised herself by finding the courage to confront him. Miserable, she returned to her vision of herself as a prisoner. Dr. Fellows, a kindly soul, had thoughtfully brought her two new books from his library; one about pirates and buried treasure and the other a history book of Captain Cook's travels to the islands. The thought of reading them bored her. Why couldn't her father understand that she desired the company of other children, to live a real life rather than this one of solitude? She remembered reading a story about an unhappy boy who had run away to have a great adventure and she wondered if she could do the same. She laughed to herself thinking how they'd never find her. Nurse would be furious. But she thought sadly, if they caught me, they would lock me in and I would be even more the prisoner than I am now.

Later Nurse came up with her night medicines and brought some of Mrs. Morimoto's little lemon cakes that she usually enjoyed. "Nurse, I asked Father if I could go home with him to Honolulu, but he didn't answer. What do you think?" Nurse was unused to Cassandra asking her such questions so she thought long and hard, as Cassandra had hoped she would and she heard, *Why would this child ask me such a thing? What should I say to her? I don't believe she is any stronger than she was last year and Honolulu can't be healthy for her.* Instead Nurse said, "I don't know about that, but I do think going into the garden every day and sketching for a little while would do you good. How would you like to do that tomorrow?" Cassandra nodded and searched Nurse's mind for more information, but none came.

That night the Menehune came to her dreams again, this time in her own garden. An older couple she hadn't seen before came towards her. The little man took her left hand and the matching little woman took the other and escorted her over to a little stone which peeked out from under a vine. The man held the vine back with one hand and brushed the dirt and dead leaves away with the other. As the woman held her hand tightly, Cassandra knelt to look closely and saw an inscription. The writing appeared very old and worn, like some Celtic characters she had seen before in the library downstairs. When she tried to ask the little people about its meaning, they began giggling and ran off. She woke up in her dark bedroom. She found herself becoming annoyed with these dreams. She reached for her pad and pen and began writing every detail she could remember. The moonlight barely provided enough light for her to see, but she discovered it didn't matter because the words flew onto the paper without any effort. Finally, she lay down on her pillow, exhausted from her efforts.

6

N urse found her exactly as she had laid down to
sleep, notebook and pencil on her bed, and
quickly let her patient know it didn't make her happy.
"Cassandra. What's this, were you writing in the dark?
What is this scribbling anyway? Surely not one of Mr.
Hunter's lessons." She continued to fuss under her
breath as she arranged the things on the desk. Cassandra
closed her eyes and wished she would vanish. "Nurse,
may I have my breakfast now, please?"

Nurse frowned and thought. *Now what is this child
up to? Scribbling in the night, such nonsense.* "Today
young lady, I have a surprise. For the first time you
may walk downstairs, have your breakfast in the dining
room, and then sketch in the garden. Evidently,
whatever you discussed with your father made quite an
impression, and I have instructions to make some
significant changes around here. You'll see."

Cassandra jumped out of bed when she heard that.
"We are? I may? Right now? Oh my goodness, where is
my shirt and my outside hat? Come on Nurse, let's go."
Hastily assembled, they began their descent. Cassandra
required Nurse's help down the stairs because she never
walked up or down the stairs by herself. Mr. Morimoto,
the gardener, or some other adult would carry her
downstairs. Although allowed to walk downstairs
today, Nurse informed her that she wouldn't be walking
up. As they reached the first floor, Nurse said,
"Walking up three flights would exhaust you, and if I

31

have anything to say about it, we will make changes one step at a time." Nurse smiled at her own joke as she went off to the kitchen to prepare her medicines.

Alone in the dining room, with its long narrow laced-lined windows which faced the garden, Cassandra stared at the oatmeal and fruit in front of her. The food did not interest her, as her thoughts centered on all that had occurred in the last few days. First, her dream, finding out about The Gift, and speaking to her father about attending school. Of course, she acknowledged he didn't promise anything, but at least today she enjoyed her breakfast downstairs. This clearly was progress. Something caught her eye just outside the open louvered windows. A dragonfly, with translucent lime-green wings, prepared to join her. She smiled and said, "Little dragonfly, welcome. Please come in, although I don't think you will enjoy oatmeal. Come join me for breakfast." As if he could hear her, the dragonfly came in the open window and buzzed around the room, pausing briefly to perch on the chair across from her. Fascinated, when she looked up and out the window behind him, she saw four more dragonflies hovering throughout the garden. Her breakfast partner made a strange noise, like a signal, and they vanished. She shook her head and wondered if she had seen them at all. Lately, magical things seemed more likely than ever before.

The idea growing in her mind, which became more of a reality every day, led her to believe that she could make something happen, rather than waiting for things to happen to her. Instead of just listening to someone's thoughts, perhaps she could actually begin to control what they said or did. She felt awakened as if before now she only existed – exactly like the mechanical doll Father brought from the mainland. She took orders and obeyed everyone in every way, and never thought for herself, let alone took action. Now she felt excitement over the prospect of creating a real life for herself.

After she finished breakfast, she exited through the kitchen into the garden. Tall, thick palms lined this entrance to the garden and in front of them were three rows of flowers all of various heights. She thought they created a multicolored skirt for the palms. She began her search for the little stone in the dream at the starting point of the footpath that ran through the entire garden. Not rushing, but taking her time, she deliberately walked past the many varieties of lilies lined in their in neat beds, the hibiscus bushes arranged by color and the red and white plants from Africa, which resembled candy canes. After the orchids, the garden's center contained mostly older and much taller tropical trees. Ferns provided thick undergrowth and vines made their home up above, reaching from the ground upwards. The dense vines provided pockets, which looked to her like little shelters. A perfect place to hide an old marker, she thought. She peeked in, expecting to see nothing, and suddenly felt the heat and the perspiration running down her face. Unsure of whether this spot resembled the one in the dream she stepped farther and farther back into the tangle of vines. She heard Nurse calling her to come to the house. Irritated that she had wasted her precious time in the garden, she sulked back to the house and allowed Mr. Morimoto to carry her upstairs. Nurse followed behind, scolding her nonstop about overexerting herself and what was she thinking and so on. Cassandra stopped listening.

As she lay on her bed in her room, she thought maybe Nurse was right. Earlier, as she came into the house from the garden, she heard Nurse's thoughts. *Her father thought this seemed like such a good idea, but goodness, just look at her. I wouldn't be surprised if she faints. If anything happens to her, it will be my fault and he'll send me packing, that's for sure.* Cassandra felt little tears welling up in her eyes. Why is this so difficult? Why can't I simply be normal like the other children? What is the worst that could happen? Now scolding herself, she returned to focus on her Latin worksheets rather than her unanswered questions.

The only subject Mr. Hunter didn't teach her was religion. Mr. Mister, the Methodist minister, would visit weekly to oversee her Bible lessons. Of course, that wasn't his name, but that's what she always called him. As a child, she thought Nurse had called him Mr. Mister instead of minister and thereafter that was his name. Cassandra liked Mr. Mister even more than she liked Mr. Hunter. He was older, but with clear blue eyes and a face that always had a ready smile for her, like a loving gracious uncle. Similar to how she imagined God actually, more loving and gentle than anything. She thought there may be a way she could ask him what he thought about The Gift, of course without divulging anything. She waited for him at her desk, watching the waves work themselves into a frenzy, shifting the deep blue color of stillness into a foamy green. Off in the distance she could see the mountains reveal their deepest carpets of green.

7

She heard Mr. Mister come in and greet Nurse and although Cassandra couldn't hear the words, she knew that he inquired about her patient's health and she had answered him. She also surmised Nurse didn't exactly paint a rosy picture. She waited to hear his footsteps. Finally, he entered the room, huffing a bit because unlike the others he carried a bit more around his middle. She knew he had children and she imagined them all lined up and neatly dressed, with their hair combed-ready for Sunday service. She thought there were at least six but she couldn't remember.

"Good morning Cassandra," he squeaked out between huffs of breath.

"Good morning Mr. Mister. Please come in and sit down. I have been waiting for you. If you don't mind I have some questions before we start the Bible lesson." Surprised, he took his seat across from Cassandra's and wiped his face and baldhead with a thin, worn handkerchief. He thought, *I wonder what has caused all of these changes, could she be getting better or is the child simply lonely and creating trouble for her own amusement?* Cassandra was shocked to hear his true feelings, but as she had given this conversation much thought, she forged ahead anyway. "Yes, well before I get to my questions I wonder if you would tell me about your children. You haven't mentioned them lately."

"That's what you want to know?" Mr. Mister smiled. "That's simple. If you recall, I have seven children, and all of them have biblical names." He thought a minute and said, "There's Ruth, she's the oldest, named after her grandmother. Then along came Mary and then Matthew, Mark, Luke, John and Paul after myself. I named the boys purposely so that I would never forget their names or their order." He laughed at his own joke.

"And where do they go to school?"

"At the village school, of course."

"But who teaches them?"

"Different teachers, of course. You know Mr. Hunter, but they are all in different rooms because they are all in different grades." He could see her frown only deepen with this information.

"I see, thank you. You know I don't know much how a school works." She paused and thought before she began again. "Mr. Mister, if someone could do something very unusual, for example, if they knew what another person was thinking or what someone was going to say before they said it, would it be a sin to use that ability?"

Mr. Mister looked at her now more curious than ever and thought *I don't like the sound of this at all. Has an evil spirit gotten a hold of her?* Cassandra couldn't help but reflect surprise on her face when she heard his thought. "Of course not," popped out of her mouth in response to his thought before she even knew it.

"Now Cassandra calm down and tell me what all this mystery questioning is about. What are you hiding? Come clean now, you know you can trust me." As he leaned in close to her, she thought his blue eyes looked straight into her soul, and he most certainly knew her thoughts. Cassandra couldn't tolerate their intensity. She took a deep breath, and said "Oh Mr. Mister, so much has happened and in less than a week. I had a strange dream about the little people, you know, the Menehune, then I had an even stranger dream and I swallowed a little dragon and then the next day I could tell what people were thinking and now I think I can make them say whatever I want. To attend a school and be with other children is all I want, Mr. Mister. Please tell me, do you think I am wrong to try to make it happen?" She stopped, out of breath and looking at him expectantly for his answer. He stood up, his face red and wet with sweat, looking for the right words. His face frightened her terribly and she began to speak but he interrupted her.

"No, Cassandra, enough. No more of this foolishness, of these ideas. Get your Bible lesson right now. I want you to ...." He droned on giving her extra assignments. Confused, she began writing his directives and wondering what she had done to make him so cross. His manner continued for the remainder of the lesson, but before he left he looked at her strangely. She hadn't heard his thoughts during the lesson but now she heard, *This must stop immediately. I will go and speak to her father right away.* To Cassandra he said, "Young lady, no more of this. You are knocking on the Devil's front door and I don't want to hear any more of this talk about reading minds. Understood?" He didn't wait for her response, walked out the door and down the stairs.

Stunned, Cassandra sat at her desk. What should she do, not tell anyone the truth? Puzzled and upset, tears slipped down her face. Haven't I been a good and obedient child? Haven't I always done what Nurse, Father and Doctor asked me to do? She thought she could use a mother right now. She tried to remember hers, not an easy task since she was so young when she died. Although she had seen pictures, smell held the strongest memory of all. Cassandra smiled. Even now when she thought of her mother, she thought of roses, old-fashioned sweet roses, faint, not overpowering like the perfume Mrs. Morimoto put on for church on Sundays. She didn't have a mother to ask, but she wondered what her mother would think, would she have sympathy for Cassandra's troubles? She decided asking questions only upset everyone, first Mr. Hunter and now Mr. Mister.

As a person beginning to know her own mind, Cassandra made a decision not to listen to other's thoughts anymore since it only caused trouble for her. Satisfied with her new resolution, she sat back in her chair and closed her eyes.

8

For the next few days, she did exactly that. She walked in the garden every day, and whenever she met Nurse, or Mr. Morimoto she would read their thoughts, and then immediately shut it off. Practice paid off because she became very good at it. For the first time in a week, she had a sense of accomplishment. Especially when she hadn't spent much time on her schoolwork.

In spite of Mr. Hunter's strong admonishment before departing the previous week, and her good intentions, she wrote in her journal during study time and didn't complete one lesson. In the past, she had done only enough work so that he wouldn't notice, but this time she had clearly earned his displeasure and he expressed it. "I am afraid I am going to have to report this disobedience to your father." Mr. Hunter's face twisted with anger and his stern, loud voice matched it. "This won't do at all, especially since I have heard you want to go to school. With this kind of performance, you won't succeed. You will be ridiculed or worse, they will think you are stupid." Now he stood and his voice grew louder as he walked toward the open door, almost as if he wanted Nurse to hear him. "Yes, next week *must* be better." He thought to himself, *Or I'll see to it that you get a whipping if that's what it takes.* Cassandra glared at him, angry that he would threaten her even in his private thoughts, her decision to stop reading thoughts forgotten. Mr. Hunter stomped down the stairs without saying anything else.

Nurse came up almost immediately, and it was obvious she had received his negative report. "Now what?" She stood in front of Cassandra with a look of disbelief on her face, and demanded in a high pinched voice, "Get your books out right now and get these lessons done. Immediately, Cassandra." Cassandra looked up at her and thought very hard, *Tell Cassandra it is all right, she doesn't have to get her work done right now*. Nurse stopped as if someone had poked her, paused and then looked down at her. "Well, on second thought, it's all right Cassandra, you don't have to get it done right now. I will go see about getting tea sent up to you." With that, Nurse turned and marched right down the stairs. Cassandra clapped her hands in joy and surprise. It did work – she had done it. Satisfied, she thought smugly, *is there anything I can't do now?* She went over to lay on her stomach and look out the window that showed the treetops of the garden. I have time to practice before Father's next visit and then I will make him tell me I can go to a school, and not on Maui, at home on Oahu. He wouldn't know she had planted the idea in his mind. She laid there for a long time planning and didn't even hear Nurse bring up the tea.

That night Cassandra had the strangest dream of all. She opened her eyes to see the same little dragon she thought she had swallowed flying around her room and lighting up the darkness with his gold-green light. The light seemed to come from his body, reflected off his wings and lit up the walls with color. At first, she lay quite still and then slowly she sat up, not wanting to scare him. She opened her hand as if inviting him to land, and whispered, "What is your name little dragon? Please come over here where I can see you." The dragon stopped its swooping over the room and slowly landed on her open palm, his wings flapping back and forth. Cassandra didn't know if she was dreaming or not, but as she looked at him he looked back at her with his head cocked to one side. She heard a tiny voice that sounded like little wings rustling; *You are a pretty girl and I like you. Ask me for anything you want anything at all and I will get it for you.* Cassandra rubbed her eye with her other hand and thought this must be a dream.

No, she heard, *you aren't dreaming and you are right, you can hear my thoughts. You see? We don't have to speak aloud to understand each other, Cassandra.*

A funny thing, thinking without speaking, but she tried it: *Can you help me get out of this house and get Father to allow me to go to school?* It felt strange to speak without moving her mouth, but he nodded in understanding.

Of course, but you don't need me for that – all you have to do is have your father say the words and I believe you already know how to do that.

Cassandra laughed. *Well, yes, I guess I do. What is your name little one?*

I like my friends to call me Pinao Ula for dragonfly. It is a little joke you see, dragon – fly. I came tonight to show you the power you have had all along. All you had to do was use it, and remember, always use it wisely.

Suddenly her eyes began closing, and she could feel herself falling asleep. She thought to the Pinao Ula, *Please, I need to sleep now. There's a lot to do in the morning.* As she opened her eyes, she saw that he had disappeared. She immediately fell into a deep sleep.

The next few days she diligently studied her lessons. She worked on her Latin and mathematics lessons as well as her map drawings. Her father had told her she would make an excellent cartographer because when she copied the old sea maps she did so perfectly. She already had one finished, ready to apply onto a globe her father had bought. She took her daily walks in the garden and began a catalog of the current plants, using the heavy botany books that were in her grandmother's library. She continued her search for the little stone the Menehune had shown her in the garden, and although she felt that it was there, she couldn't find it. Dreams are mysterious and although she tried to replicate the markings on the stone as soon as she awoke, she could never make any sense of it.

She asked Mr. Hunter for some books on the Menehune, claiming she wanted to know more about Hawaiian folklore and he eagerly agreed, anxious to take her mind off her strange questions of late. He had to request the books from the library and it might be a while for them to arrive, but Cassandra didn't mind. She now had a real plan.

The little dragon hadn't returned, but she could be patient now that she knew it wasn't a dream and that both the dragon and The Gift were real. Cassandra had thought her plan through. She would have her father say that he considered this for some time, and he agreed it would be good for her to attend school on Oahu. As it was almost the summer, she could start in the fall. She comforted herself that planting thoughts like this couldn't be wrong, and it couldn't be a sin. She would feel bad about purposely sinning, but she didn't feel bad, she felt happy and excited with the thought of being with other children.

The day came for her father's return. She awoke confident that he would have good reports from Nurse and Mr. Hunter because she had worked extra hard on her lesson. Every day she walked in the garden, worked on her catalog of plants and flowers, and took care not to become tired or overheated. She had become obedient again.

As she walked downstairs to join her father and Dr. Fellows for the long-awaited examination she smiled. Things were proceeding as planned. As she entered the room, she saw them in their usual positions, with their teacups on the table. She concentrated as hard as she could on her first step, planting the idea in the doctor's mind so that he would find her fit enough to go to regular school. That was the last thing she remembered because she dropped to the floor in a dead faint. As she awoke, she knew immediately what had happened. Her father and Dr. Fellows had called Nurse and everyone had panicked. Cassandra also panicked at the thought of not being able to carry out her plan. How could she execute it now? She jumped to her feet quickly, saying,

"This has not happened before, I promise. I don't know why it happened, but please, listen to me all of you, I am fine."

She heard her father's thought, *I guess that's the end of any chance of her going home to Oahu and going to school and staying with me.* He stood up from where he had been kneeling next to her and walked to the doorway, calling for Mrs. Morimoto to bring some tea and biscuits for her, and directing Nurse to get the tonic. Cassandra felt lightheaded as she allowed the impact of her father's thought to sink in. Wonderful, truly wonderful, not all is lost then, and even better than attending school on Maui, Father had been thinking of taking her home to Oahu. She was recalibrating quickly now. If he already had that thought then it shouldn't be too hard to get him to say it aloud. She steadied her nerves, focused on her father, and projected the thought: *Cassandra, I have decided that you need to come home to Oahu with me and go to school.*

Her father looked startled and half turned around looking to see if someone had pinched him from behind. Cassandra giggled to herself. He looked straight at her, "Cassandra come over here." She stood up and walked deliberately to where he was standing. "Cassandra, I have been giving this a great deal of thought," but his words and thoughts were so loud and mixed up she put up her hand, to signal him to wait a minute, and then consciously turned off her "listening mind" which is how she thought of it. "Sorry Father, ready now, as you were saying?" she prompted.

"Yes, well, in spite of what just happened here, Dr. Fellows, Nurse and I have been discussing your case and we all believe you would be better off at home with me. I plan on closing up this house and taking you back to Oahu." Sweat beaded up on his forehead and as the trades had cooled the room, she wondered if her fainting had scared him. She searched his face to read his thoughts and she heard something amazing, *What if she died too? She might as well be at home, rather than shut up in this old house.* Never in a million years did she think her father capable of such a thought, and she honestly didn't care why because as a result she had her wish come true. As calm as she could she said, "Father, I know that my fainting scared you, but this news has made me the happiest girl. How soon can we leave?"

Her father sighed, "We have already begun the arrangements, but it will take at least three more weeks before we can be packed and ready to leave for Oahu. Your school records and release must be prepared, and I will return to oversee the packing, close the house and take care of Mr. and Mrs. Morimoto. For now, Nurse will return with us." He paused and added, "Do you think you can be helpful here for the next three weeks?"

"Of course, Father." Cassandra's voice reflected her true excitement over this news. She didn't care that she didn't execute her plan as she had hoped because this turn of events exceeded all of her expectations.

9

Time no longer dragged on for Cassandra as the moving activity consumed the household. She had almost finished her garden catalogs to take along to Oahu. She began a new secret journal with drawings of all of the Menehune she had met in her dreams and of course, her little dragon friend. The steamer trunks stood packed and ready, when one afternoon she heard Mr. Mister's voice downstairs. Cassandra had not seen him since the day he had spoken to her so sharply. He asked Nurse to send her to the garden. He waited for her on the little stone bench in front of the large gardenia bush heavy with pungent white flowers.

"Ah, Cassandra, sit down." He wiped his forehead with his handkerchief. She sat, a little hesitantly. Although a few weeks had passed since their last exchange, the hurt remained fresh. She had thought of him as friend and confidante.

"Cassandra," he said, taking her hand gently and looking intently at her, his ocean-blue eyes instantly reminding her of how much she cared for him. "Please don't be angry with me for leaving the way I did a few weeks ago. I am here to explain my reason for being so upset, but before I do; what I tell you must remain between us, no one else is to know, do you understand?" She nodded, wondering how she could promise such a thing before she had even heard it. Mr. Mister took a deep breath and began, "Long ago, another little girl lived in this very house, born to your grandparents, born before your father."

"Why don't I know about her?" Cassandra asked, "There are no pictures anywhere of an aunt."

"I know, please let me explain and then you can ask questions, all right?"

"Yes, sir." She complied. "Cassandra, the girl was beautiful and beloved by everyone, including me who knew her from childhood. Before I left for the seminary we became engaged and planned to marry when I returned." Sensing that she had a question he held up his hand, "Please, this is very difficult for me, all right? I have never told this to anyone before, so let me continue. Right before I went to the mainland for my seminary training, I came to see her. In fact, exactly in the same spot where we sit now. Barely 18, I told her my concern, that a young woman of her spirit may not wish to wait for my return, and that I would understand if she didn't want to keep our engagement. I didn't wish for her to be lonely and unhappy. That's when she told me her secret. She wouldn't be lonely because she had the Menehune and they visited her and kept her company with their stories." Cassandra gasped but clasped her hand over her mouth so that he would continue.

"Cassandra, I grew up on the islands and knew of the Menehune stories, but I immediately concluded it to be Satan's work. She patiently explained that since she was a child she had known the Menehune and they had shared with her the secret of knowing another's thoughts." He paused, watching her face intently before he continued.

"I became angry and I shouted at her to stop the fantasy, that clearly the Menehune could only be the work of Satan and his dark evil spirits. I further told her to get down on her knees and ask God to save her from demon possession." He stopped and wiped the tears from his eyes, unable to continue. He took a deep breath, wiped his face again and continued looking at his hands in his lap. "As I said, I was very angry with her, Cassandra, and I said that unless she repented immediately and asked God to heal her of this demon possession I would break our engagement. My zeal for purity, my youth, and lack of understanding blinded me to her tears as she pleaded with me to listen to her. She explained that she couldn't repent because they had saved her from loneliness, and they were her friends. I stood up and left her standing there and walked away without looking back." Here he hesitated, "And now I am sorry, so sorry to tell you the rest of the story." He stood up and walked over to the tall, flowering hibiscus bushes lining the other side of the footpath. "Come," he said, "I want to show you something." She followed him, now worried about the end of his story.

"May I ask a question while we walk?"

He sighed, "Yes, what is it?"

"Well, if your story is true about my aunt, what was her name, and why doesn't anyone talk about her anymore? The Captain and Grandmother died, but Father speaks of them and there are lots of pictures of them."

"Follow me," he said again and soon he stopped beside the large yellow hibiscus bush near the hot pink one she loved the most. He reached down and pulled back the ferns that had grown over the path. She held her breath in amazement as she saw the same stone she had seen in her dream. "You see?" he said. "This is the marker they placed here after she died. Her parents, your grandparents, wired me shortly after I began my studies at seminary on the mainland. They must not have known about the last conversation we had, about the last time I saw her. Anyway, they wired me to say that she hadn't eaten and had taken to her bed. They called in all sorts of doctors to heal her, but no one could. Finally they called in a Kupuna, or old wise one, from the village for help because she wouldn't tell anyone what was wrong, or why she had taken to her bed." Again, he paused; she waited breathlessly for him to continue.

"The old woman asked to be left alone with her and after a long while came out and told them that she was dying from a broken heart. Your grandparents didn't know about our last conversation or that I had broken the engagement. Only I knew that my heartlessness had killed her. I alone bore the blame. She died the next day and that's when they wired me.

"Your grandparents were a forgiving people and I owed them an explanation, but to add to my sins I did something worse. Although I did write and tell them how we had quarreled and I had ended the engagement, and that the blame for her death lay at my feet, I committed a sin of omission. I never told them why we had quarreled and perhaps that's why the Menehunes have come back to haunt me through you. Someone wants to remind me that I remain guilty of breaking Nellie's heart."

He sat abruptly and began weeping, holding his head in his hands. "In spite of their own despair at losing their daughter, being good Christian parents, they promptly wrote me and granted me forgiveness. I understand they removed all pictures of their daughter so as not be reminded of their loss. After seminary, I hoped for an assignment on the mainland, anywhere but Hawaii, but all of the church assignments kept pointing me back to the islands. Finally, ten years ago I accepted the assignment here.

"When I arrived, I learned that your grandparents had both recently died. Your father knew of his sister and that she had been engaged, but he didn't know that I was her fiancé. He was too young at the time. Of course, others knew, but no one mentioned it out of kindness at my shame. You know the rest. After attending college on the mainland your father married and settled in his practice in Honolulu. I tried to forget and in spite of my old age a local girl agreed to marry me and yes, I know you know the rest." He stopped suddenly, spent from spilling his painful secret.

She searched his thoughts and heard nothing but sorrow and remorse. "Mr. Mister, why do you tell me this now?"

"I don't wish to make another mistake Cassandra. I didn't want to accuse you as I did her because I have paid for it with a guilty conscience my whole life and here you are with a bad heart and I hurt you, just as I hurt her. All I could see was her voice and her words when you were telling me what you thought you could do." He stood up and once again wiped the tears from his face. "Now you are moving back to Oahu and away from this house and I, for one, am happy for you. It is good for you to have a chance to have a life of your own with other children and not be shut up in this house where you imagine you can read the thoughts of others and worse things."

Cassandra felt suddenly very much older than her ten years and she felt very sorry for him. "Mr. Mister, these are things that happened a long time ago," she began, "and you couldn't have known what would happen. Please don't worry about me. I possess a large imagination and perhaps you are correct, I have been spending too much time with fantasy stories and not enough with real life." He nodded, but then he stopped. What had she meant by he "was correct?" Surely, he hadn't uttered that thought aloud. He shook his head to dismiss the idea and walked toward the house, now emptied of the burden he no longer carried. He had confessed, not to another minister or to a trusted confidant, but to this girl, the niece of the woman he had loved and whose heart he had broken.

Cassandra heard his thoughts as he walked away from her without a final farewell, *Did I save Cassandra from a similar fate? Is she involved with the Menehune or the spirit world? Will this move to Oahu allow her to focus on her life in the present, rather than in the world of dreams and fantasy?* He comforted himself by thinking that he had done all he could do. *Now it is up to God to save her.*

Cassandra stood in front of the stone and this time she could see the writing she couldn't in her dream. It was the same stone; strange that she had never seen it before, off to the side of the footpath. She pulled back the ferns again and there it was:

> Nellie Rose Bartholomew
> Born January 17, 1895
> Died October 12, 1915
> Beloved daughter, gone too soon.

Her eyes swam with tears and she sat on the nearby bench. What did this all mean? Why had no one ever mentioned this much beloved aunt? Did it shame the family that Nellie Rose died of a broken heart? Did Mr. Mister share all of the story's details? She considered asking her father but there would surely be more questions, such as how did she know this. And she had promised Mr. Mister she wouldn't say a word.

Amazed at the prospect of dying from a broken heart, she slowly got up and made her way back to the house. She saw Nurse watching her out the window and heard her wondering, *Now what has gotten into her today? How strange. She is no longer with Mr. Mister, and he left without saying a word to me.*

Then Cassandra thought, maybe no one else knows about Nellie Rose. Maybe Father doesn't even know if she died before he was old enough to remember. She started the long climb up to her room. In preparation for returning home her father wanted her to climb, but she had to promise to stop and count to 100 at each landing.

10

The days passed quickly as Cassandra anxiously awaited moving day. She had overheard Mrs. Morimoto's thoughts, more troubling than she cared to admit. The old woman was packing some dishware, and Cassandra heard sadness in her thoughts. *I am going to miss living in the house, and after all, I have lived in it over fifty years. Mr. Bartholomew lost a large case, which affected his reputation, so I understand his money troubles and why he can no longer keep two houses and house help. What will happen to my Cassandra? How will she survive the dampness of the Manoa Valley?* Mrs. Morimoto paused as she heard Cassandra behind her and scolded her for startling her, "You know it's not polite to sneak up behind someone. I could have dropped a dish and broke it." Instead of responding, Cassandra asked, "What will you and Mr. Morimoto do now that we won't be here in the house anymore?"

Now her look softened and she smiled, "Oh, don't worry about us, our family has a large farm on the Big Island and we will go there and help them." Cassandra sighed. She hugged Mrs. Morimoto impulsively and said, "I will miss you. You know I can't remember living anywhere else and my life won't be the same without you."

Now back to her stoic self, Mrs. Morimoto said, "Yes, yes and I will miss you too. Now go and get me more wrapping paper so that I can finish."

Oahu

Two days later Cassandra, dressed in her traveling clothes, readied herself for the brief voyage to Oahu. She waved nervously to Mr. and Mrs. Morimoto as they drove away from the house. She looked back at the house as long as she could so she would remember.

The thought of being on a ship and seeing Oahu from the sea thrilled her and made her think of when pirates approached a new island. She couldn't remember anything about the harbor or her home in Manoa. Her entire knowledge consisted of the fact that it was a large house, she would have a room on the second floor, and she wouldn't be able to see the ocean anymore.

Her father, quite serious the entire trip, spoke mostly to Nurse in low tones and didn't pay Cassandra much attention. For some strange reason he allowed her to stay out on the deck in the sea air. She hoped to see dolphins or whales as she could from her window at home, but a crewmember laughed at her when she asked. "Listen sister, that's not this time of year, come back later."

"Oh." she said, embarrassed. Soon they were at the port and while her father supervised the unloading of their trunks, she walked beside Nurse to the automobiles waiting for them. *Perhaps Mrs. Morimoto was wrong and Father is not in any kind of trouble. Surely, he wouldn't have brought them here if that were the case,* but a little thought kept nagging her. The night before she had trouble sleeping. The excitement of the move, or perhaps something else altogether. She thought she had a dream about her little dragon friend, Pinao Ula, but it evaporated like a mist when she awoke. With the present bombarding her senses, she pushed the dream from her mind. The smells demanded her attention instead. She had not been near the ocean for a long time and the port smelled of spices, fish and people, all sorts of different people. Her imagination ran wild with the stories she had read of seafaring men, including her grandfather. She tried to picture him on a ship. Had he been serious and severe like that man on the ship docked over there, or was he kind like the captain she had met on their ship? She noted that their ship resembled more of a ferry than a serious sea-going vessel. She saw few children, mostly older, and quite serious in their demeanor, not welcoming at all.

They settled into the two vehicles and began the trip to Manoa. She watched out the window the entire time, her mouth open with wonder at the shops and people, many with colorful shirts and various shoes. Typical tourists, Nurse said. As they turned to drive up to Manoa, she saw her beloved hibiscus everywhere welcoming her home. Many different plants decorated the front porches and steps of the houses they passed. Her skin felt sticky and hot and she could see some afternoon showers heading in from the ocean.

"Nurse," she turned to her longtime caregiver. "Have you been to our house before?" Nurse looked at her and thought *Now what?* Nurse sighed, "No,

Cassandra I have always worked at the house on Maui, so you see this is new to me too."

At last, they arrived at the house and a thin elderly man came out to greet them. He smiled at her and said, "Cassandra, I am very happy to see you so well and such a fine young lady."

Her father said, "Cassandra, this is Mr. Takamura. You probably don't remember him, but he will be helping us out here as he has since you were a baby." She smiled back at him and Mr. Takamura took her bag and went up the stairs into the house. "Father, may I look around for a bit?" Her father, distracted with the unpacking didn't respond, but Nurse said, "Go ahead, but be sure you come into the kitchen soon. You'll have to take your tonic as soon as it is unloaded."

The house was a large bungalow made mostly of dark Koa wood with floor to ceiling dark green louvered shutters on either side of a heavy wooden front door. Cassandra could tell from the winding hilly roads they drove to reach the house that they were higher up, but the heavy foliage blocked any possible views from the porch. The large porch protected the inside of the house from rain and allowed the shutters to remain open most of the time. The porch wrapped halfway around both sides of the house, emptying through two short staircases into the side yards. As she rounded the back of the house, she could see a screen door with a path to a kitchen garden and a large arbor overgrown with palms and other native plants, some that looked different from the Maui garden. She realized that she could actually see houses on either side and behind, a departure from the remoteness she had experienced in Maui, but she could also hear roosters, a sound familiar to her. She turned her attention back to the garden and now noticed that the kitchen herb garden was overgrown and the hibiscus were not trimmed as they were at her former home. She remembered Mrs. Morimoto's thoughts and again wondered if her father had money troubles.

She pushed the thought away and walked farther into the garden. She saw an old birdbath made of stone, long empty, stained and crumbling at the bottom. She heard something in the bushes and turned to see an enormous grayish cat with large dark gray eyes glaring at her as if she had invaded his territory. She called to it, "Hello! Well, I am sorry I invaded your garden. Won't you come here and greet me properly?" The cat turned its head and walked back into the shrub.

Cassandra thought, *what a wonderful welcome to my new home.* She heard Nurse calling and walked into the house, this time through the kitchen screen door. She let it slam loudly and found the noise quite satisfactory. *This will do for my new home after all,* she thought.

11

"Cassandra." She heard her father calling her from upstairs. As she climbed the single staircase to the second floor, she noticed it wasn't as narrow as in Maui. It was made of the same Koa wood as the rest of the house, but the center was a lighter color, shiny from use. She reached the top of the landing and turned because she knew her room would face the street. As she came into the bedroom, her father stood there wearing an uncomfortable, forced smile. "Well, how do you like it? Once it served as your nursery, but I do think Mr. Takamura and I did a fair job fixing it up for a girl your age, what do you think?" The walls and trim wore various shades of lavender, the color of early spring flowers. Sparkling white ruffled curtains hung on two large square windows facing the street, with a window seat nestled directly below. An embroidered cushion of white and purple flowers topped the window seat, creating a special place for her to read. She walked over to touch it, sat on the seat, and looked out the window. Her heart leaped. She did have a view after all. Houses topped with various rooftops and thick tropical greenery graced the sloping hillside to the city. She stood and twirled around, "Oh Father, I cannot tell you how beautiful I find this. I believe that I am going to love it here. Thank you, thank you for allowing me to return home." It would have been appropriate to hug her father at that moment, but she hung back and instead formulated the question she wanted to ask him.

He interrupted her thoughts. "Cassandra, there's something I need to tell you. I, well, actually there's someone coming to see you in a few days. I doubt that you remember her, but she is your grandmother. In fact, you were named for her." She absorbed this new fact by saying her name to herself, Cassandra Leora Bartholomew. He saw her puzzled face and added, "She is your mother's mother, Cassandra, and she is hoping that you will be able to spend some time with her up at her house in Nuuanu Valley, as I will be quite busy with this new case of mine. You know," then he stopped and coughed and she read his thought, *how can I tell her that there will be more change?* "Cassandra, there's more, more changes, that is. For the rest of the summer Nurse will only be here during the week, and now that you are older she will no longer stay the night. I, well, I hope you don't find that upsetting."

She stared at him. "Is it because we don't have any money to pay her, Father?"

"What? Where did you hear that?" He almost spit the words out.

"I didn't exactly hear it, but since we couldn't keep Mr. and Mrs. Morimoto on anymore and closed up the Maui house, and then I heard it might be sold and..." To her dismay, large drops began to roll down her cheeks, the result of keeping a secret for so long. "Please Father, just tell me the truth. I am old enough to know the truth." And she looked up at him, waiting.

"Goodness, come over here." He held out his arms and awkwardly tried to hold her, something he hadn't done before. He sat down on the bed as she stood in front of him and looked her straight in the eyes. "Cassandra, this is a difficult thing for me to say to you. I had a very important case, actually a murder case. I do hope you understand that is what I do for a living?" She nodded. "Well, the case didn't go well, and as the defense attorney I didn't get the case dismissed or even a lesser charge of manslaughter and a great many people were angry with me."

Finally, someone shared the truth with her. "Please tell me what happened, Father."

"A wealthy young man from one of the oldest families on the island became romantically involved with a young local girl against the wishes of his parents. There was a terrible accident involving a lover's quarrel, and a gun. The young man died. His parents demanded justice and my job was to defend the young woman, and prove that it was simply an accident. New evidence introduced by the prosecutor at the last minute threw doubt on our argument that it was an accident. Now, a good defense attorney can deal with the unexpected, but I couldn't compete with an unexpected credible witness who planted doubt about my client's innocence. In fact, I remain convinced, that the young man had actually intended to kill my client. In any event, the young woman's family and others are angry about the guilty conviction and they believe that it has something to do with the boy's wealthy parents. The reason the case affects us is that my reputation as a criminal defense attorney is on the line, Cassandra. No one wants to hire a lawyer who loses. I can see you are already worried, please don't be. That case ended some time ago and although I haven't had a lot of paying clients, I have one now. It's a very different case for me. My client needs to settle her family's estate and I am being paid quite well, so please stop worrying." He stood up and led her toward the door. "Now down to business. Because I will be spending a lot of time on this case, your grandmother is anxious for you to spend time with her. Promise me that you will rest as much as you should when you are with her, and if you experience even one fainting spell you must return home at once so that we can contact Dr. Fellows. Do you understand?" Cassandra nodded obediently although she couldn't imagine how being with an old woman would be a concern.

"School begins in a month's time and we have an appointment so that you can meet the principal and perhaps your teacher. You are not nervous about starting school with other children, are you? I did consider getting a tutor to come to the house so you wouldn't have to go to school at all."

She interrupted him, although she knew that it equated to poor manners. "Father, please. I know how to take care of myself, and I am nearly 11. You know I won't do anything silly to cause me to faint or become overtired. Being with other children is exactly what I want."

"All right for now." He checked his watch, and prepared to leave. "I have to get back to the office for a bit. I will be back for supper and I expect to hear that you have unpacked and are settled in."

So much to think about Cassandra thought as she sank down on the window seat and reviewed everything that her father had shared. Her grandmother? What kind of a family never talks about those it loses or those who are still alive? Why had she never received a letter from her grandmother? Cassandra considered her father's story of the case he had lost, and found herself losing faith in anything people told her. In these past few weeks, her life had turned topsy-turvy and her mind opened to so many new revelations. Omissions of truth or mistruths. Whom could she believe?

Still the good girl, she unpacked her trunks and set about arranging her room with special attention to her writing desk. She arranged her writing utensils and as she placed her writing paper on her desk, a small colored envelope fell to the floor. Curiously, she picked it up. It was sealed with a gold wax seal, the kind she had read about in books of the middle ages. *Who uses those anymore?* Her hands shook as she opened it and sat down to read it.

Dear Cassandra,

I know you are going to leave and study in Oahu, but I must warn you. You have read classical literature and books others may consider archaic. The children you meet may laugh at your word choices and your manner of speech.

Please don't let them upset you. It is only because you have spent much of the past five years learning Latin and reading many of our ancient manuscripts that at times your speech resembles someone from the middle ages rather than a modern girl. My advice to you is to listen and learn from the others before you speak.

I wish you only the best and many blessings on your future life.

Your teacher,
Nathan Hunter.

Another revelation, just when she thought she had seen enough. She tucked the note into her dress pocket and went downstairs for tea. Nurse cast her a strange look as she entered the kitchen. "Has your father told you that I won't be here anymore in the evening or on the weekends?"

"He did." Cassandra said, picking a grape off the dessert plate.

"Well," Nurse asked, "Are you going to be all right here by yourself at night?

"What do you mean by myself? Father will be here." She heard Nurse's thoughts, *Silly girl; she's never been alone in a house before. How does she know she will be all right? I am so angry with her father I can't see straight and sending her up to Nuuanu Valley, ridiculous, not to mention dangerous.*

"Do you know my grandmother?" Cassandra asked, anxious to get Nurse onto another subject, and wanting to know more about Nuuanu Valley.

"No, I do not, but I have heard some stories about her, perhaps simply gossip, I am sure I don't know. Come on now, and take your medicine." Cassandra stopped herself from hearing any more of Nurse's opinions and thought; I don't want to know what she or anyone else thinks. I want to find out about my grandmother for myself, and I will know soon enough.

The cook, Mr. Takamura, actually lived at the house so Nurse was incorrect about her being alone when Father had to work late or be away. She liked Mr. Takamura right away. He was a small-boned Japanese man, who always smiled at her in greeting and presented her with miniature cakes whenever she came into the kitchen. She couldn't determine his age so one day she simply asked him. "Excuse me, Mr. Takamura, but how old are you?"

He smiled at her again, his jet-black hair, streaked with silver, falling onto his forehead. "Too old to answer silly questions. I must continue working now." And he turned and resumed chopping the onions.

12

Finally, the day came when she would meet her grandmother. She ran down the stairs, knowing she shouldn't, and hurried into the kitchen where Mr. Takamura had laid out her breakfast along with her medications. She had found some clothes she thought would be appropriate for meeting her grandmother, but she had no idea what to expect. "Is Father here?" she asked Mr. Takamura.

"No, he had to leave for the office early." She thought it strange he wouldn't be here to introduce her to her grandmother. She heard a loud noise outside and ran to the screen door. A surprise greeted her. An army-green Jeep with an open top had pulled right up to the front porch steps. Nothing had prepared her for the woman at the wheel, an elegant, extremely lean woman who clearly didn't look elderly. She leapt out of the Jeep, not bothering to open the door or put the step down and bounded up the porch stairs looking through the screen at Cassandra, whose mouth had dropped open.

Dressed for riding with a blue-jean shirt, khaki pants and riding boots, her grandmother also wore a smile that spread across her face. She bent down and said, "Well, get out here and let me take a look at you. I can't believe how much you've grown since I last saw you. You were sickly then, but look at you now." She opened the door and pulled Cassandra out onto the porch. "Come on over here; let's sit and get acquainted.

Mr. T," she yelled through the door, "May I please get some tea out here?" She took Cassandra by the hand, led her to a bamboo settee, and plunked herself down next to her. "I take it from the look on your face that I am a surprise to you, correct?" Sitting very still, all Cassandra could manage was a nod. "Your father never said one word about me the whole time you were in Maui?" Again, she nodded in response. "That figures." And she slapped her knee, threw her head back, and laughed. A loud and wonderful laugh, and about the best human noise Cassandra had ever heard. "Not a surprise girl, not a surprise." Mr. Takamura came out, handed her the tea, and put some of his special cakes on the table in front of them. As he did so, he smiled and winked at Cassandra as if they shared a secret.

"I guess you have a lot of questions for me, don't you?" As she leaned into Cassandra and poured her tea, Cassandra could smell something like citrus, perhaps coming from her hair. Her hair held as much fascination as the rest of her for Cassandra. A beautiful silver, thick, shiny mass piled up on top of her head in a loose knot. Most of the ladies she had seen wore their hair braided or tightly pulled back so that it wouldn't blow in the trade winds. Her eyes appeared to be brown but contained flecks of green and gold that sparkled. At least that's what Cassandra thought she saw without staring, which she so wanted to do. Now her grandmother was across from her, leaning against the porch rail with her cup in hand and examining her granddaughter closely. "You do talk, don't you girl?"

Cassandra started to stammer and couldn't think fast enough. She sensed this was a person who would tell her the truth; who wouldn't tell her things she couldn't understand, and who would help her make sense of this world. "Uh, oh, Grandmother may I call you that?" she finally spit out.

Her grandmother frowned, "No, you definitely may not. My name is Leora and that's what you should call me."

Cassandra continued to stammer, "Very pleased to meet you, Leora, and you are correct. In Maui my father, Nurse, doctor, teacher, and minister talked about my grandparents and of course my mother. But no one ever told me about *you*."

"Yes," Leora said in response, sipping her tea. "So come on girl, what questions do you have for me?" Cassandra thought, I need to be careful and she tried to read Leora's thoughts for help. She didn't want to offend her and have her suddenly close up like so many others. She decided to start with a safe question. "Did you see me when I was little, before they sent me away?"

"Well, of course I did. Especially when your mother was sick. Actually I took care of you."

"Then you will tell me about her? Father gets misty-eyed when I ask him and won't say anything. I want to know everything. I want to know what she was like as a girl and if she had secrets and friends and everything you can tell me about her."

Leora cocked her head to one side and looked at her with a bit of puzzlement, and then she said aloud, "We are going to have lots of time to cover all of those subjects, but first I have a question for you. What exactly did you do up in the old house on Maui?"

Cassandra sighed, pained at the thought of her lonely life. "Once I felt well enough to sit up I learned to read and write. I stayed in my attic room and studied my lessons. I started reading Chaucer last year and this year Virgil, and of course, I studied my Latin diligently."

"And it's true that you want to go to school, even though you haven't taken any exams or gone to a regular school before?"

"Oh. Mr. Hunter, who was my instructor, says I will be more than capable of keeping up with the other children, although he warned me I must not be impetuous or too forward."

Leora, silent for a minute, asked, "So why do you think your father suddenly brought you back to Oahu? Is your heart better? Do you still suffer from fainting spells?"

Again, Cassandra tried to form her words carefully so as not to offend Leora, this larger-than-life effusive woman she hoped to be able to trust with all of her secrets, even the one Mr. Mister told her not to share.

Suddenly Leora frowned at her and interrupted her thoughts, "But that's not what you are going to wear today is it? Don't you own any pants, Cassandra?"

Cassandra looked down at her day dress and pinafore, something she always wore back in Maui, and said, "No, I do not."

Leora sighed, "I guess for today we can make this work, but we'll have to get you some proper clothes if you are going to spend time with me. Come on, let's get Lulubell and get this show on the road."

Now Cassandra was puzzled. *Who was Lulubell?* Leora saw her face, laughed, and pointed to her Jeep, "My sweet Lulubell," and Cassandra understood. Leora yelled through the door, "We'll be leaving now, Mr. T. Thanks for the delicious tea. I should have her back before bedtime. Don't worry about supper, she'll be having that with me."

13

L eora grabbed Cassandra's hand and led her down the stairs into the Jeep. As she pulled onto the highway Cassandra could see that she liked to drive very fast. Cassandra's lack of experience with cars only added to the excitement. Within about 30 minutes, they reached an unmarked entrance to Leora's compound. As they reached the end of the long twisted driveway, Cassandra caught a glimpse of a structure somewhat hidden at the edge of the property. It looked like a hut to Cassandra, and as they got closer, she concluded it actually was a rectangular structure patched together with metal pieces. Palm leaves lined its roof, and rivers of rust trailed down the walls. It appeared to have a front porch. A stable edged the right side of the property and a huge fenced garden lined the left. Leora jumped out of the Jeep and called, "Come on in and see the place and then we'll go for a ride." Astonished at Leora's energy, Cassandra wondered, who was this woman so full of life and power? She couldn't imagine how she could be her grandmother. As she entered the house, in the kitchen she saw an old-fashioned farm table painted yellow, with streaks of white peeking out from underneath, with two worn and mismatched chairs. Something was cooking on the metal two-burner gas stove. Leora lifted the lid and smelled it, "That's our dinner in there. Pot roast and tofu wrapped in bananas leaves; you are going to love it." She motioned for Cassandra to follow her to the front room, a large odd shaped space with a long desk on her left and a full bank of windows, floor to ceiling, in front of her. When Cassandra saw the view, she gasped. She could see all the way to the harbor and could clearly view the ships. *Like my view back on Maui, only prettier* she thought. Leora answered her thought, "Yes, similar to the one you had in Maui I'll bet, only wider and prettier, yes?"

Too shocked to say anything in response, Cassandra pushed the idea that Leora had read her thoughts out of her head. Eagerly she looked about, wanting to know more about her grandmother's life. Each wall contained a floor-to-ceiling bookcase stuffed with books. More books covered the desk, on the floor, next to tables with papers sticking out of many of them. In one corner stood a wooden carved secretary almost touching the ceiling, chock full of notes and papers. There were other old furnishings in the room. An overstuffed sofa covered with a khaki throw faced the windows, skirted by two large bamboo chairs, their green and white striped cushions worn with age. Square camp tables with strange old lamps graced every open spot. The room reminded her of a field research station she had once seen in a magazine. She noticed a number of photographs of her as a baby in various sizes and frames, stuck everywhere possible. She saw one of her mother and one with a large mustached man. She wondered if he could be her other grandfather, Leora's husband. She thought she might as well start asking questions now. "Where's a picture of grandfather, Leora? Do you have a picture I could see?"

"Goodness girl, watching you take in this room just now I see you have a curious mind. We'll look at pictures tonight after dinner and I'll fill you in on all of the family history, or perhaps you will find family gossip more interesting." Cassandra laughed and said that would be great.

Leora said, "Come on then, here's the sandwiches I fixed and some drinks. Let's take Jenny for a little ride. You are going to have to get used to this if you are going to be spending time up here with me." She quickly packed a little knapsack and walked with Cassandra out to the stable. Cassandra could see now why pants would have been a good idea. Leora walked Jenny out of the barn and tightened the saddle. "Don't you worry" Leora said. "Today we'll take it easy. You can ride in front of me and we'll slowly break you into riding. I assume you haven't ridden before?"

Somewhat embarrassed, Cassandra nodded, "That's right, I haven't."

"There's nothing to it girl." Before Cassandra could respond her grandmother quickly picked her up and swung her onto the saddle and then followed, expertly landing right behind her. "Now, you relax and leave everything to me. A good horse knows when its riders are nervous and we don't want Jenny to worry about you, so relax, you hear me?" Cassandra nodded but she was so excited she was beside herself. Just a few weeks ago she hadn't gone farther than her garden, and today she was riding a horse.

"Okay, Cassandra listen carefully to me." Leora whispered into her ear as they trotted out into the yard.

"I am going to hold onto the reins and you hold onto the saddle there and don't let go, you understand? I take paths that sometimes are rough or slick from the rains so you have to sit tight in front of me, got it?" Cassandra nodded nervously. The next hour flew by as Leora walked Jenny down the various paths of the Upper Nuuanu Valley, showing Cassandra what she had planted years ago. Many of the plants were new to Cassandra, including tobacco and bamboo so tall that she couldn't see their tops. As directed, Cassandra hung on tight, listened and leaned back into Leora and found her lean and hard and strong, not as warm and squishy as she imagined a grandmother would be. For the first time that day Cassandra felt, and here she had difficulty describing it, comfortable, or relaxed. She had never been on a horse, never been in a bamboo forest or seen lush green plants but her mind felt at ease and wasn't working hard as it usually did. She closed her eyes, smelled the moist air around her, and thought this must be what happiness feels like.

Leora had stopped talking, "Are you listening, Cassandra?"

Her eyes flew open, "Oh, I am sorry. I am so surprised at how nice it is to be here, on Oahu, with you, and on a horse. I can't believe this is all happening to me, it's like a dream."

"Look, here Cassandra, look at the butterflies straight ahead. Have you ever seen anything so beautiful? Slow, slow Jenny." Leora slowed the horse to a pause and she held out her arm in front of Cassandra. A large black and purple beauty came to rest regally still as if she had called her. "Here come some more, now you try it. Hold out your arm." Suddenly two of the huge black and purple butterflies sat on her arm so close she could look right at them. Just as quickly they decided it was time to go and one by one, each flew away and as they did, Cassandra realized she had been holding her breath and felt lightheaded.

"Grandmother, I mean Leora, do you think we could rest for a while?" She leaned back against her, now welcoming her steadiness.

"Oh yes, we are going to go over to a grassy spot to have our lunch, hold on." In a minute, they were in an open, grassy meadow, and Leora dismounted and helped Cassandra down. She quickly took the blanket she had tied onto the back of the saddle and laid out the little lunch she had brought them. Cassandra sat down, feeling dizzy. She tried to read Leora's mind again, but nothing. She sighed and thought *I have so many questions I don't know where to start.*

"Go ahead and ask those questions, girl. I'm right here waiting for you. Ask away." Leora laughed and handed her a sandwich and drink. Nothing about her grandmother would surprise her now, and as she chewed, she thought.

Finally, she said, "I think I need to start with my mother. I don't know much and while I have some pictures, I want to know more about her."

"All right, you eat and I'll talk. First of all your mother, Camilla Elizabeth, always radiated sweetness and light, and even as a baby wasn't cross or unhappy. She was one of the most content people I have ever had the pleasure of meeting in my life and I am not biased because she was my baby girl. Everyone thought the same thing. She never said a bad word about anyone, even when people were mean to her. She attended Punahou School and had many friends, as you will see from her pictures. And a real beauty too, but a bit shorter than I am. Although my hair is silver now, it used to be light golden brown, and so was hers. She especially loved to play tennis and of course, she rode often in competitions, an all-round athletic girl."

Cassandra took it all in, trying hard to imagine what her mother looked like. Leora smiled, "In those days most girls went to the mainland for college and I guess we thought that would be the best place for Camilla too. She discovered her interests were science and oceanography so after she graduated she came back home to Honolulu and that's when she met your father. After a quick romance, they were engaged and married within the year. And the next year little old *you* appeared." She stopped suddenly, "Is this what you wanted to hear?"

"Oh yes, please go on, I want to hear what happened to my mother."

"Like all new parents, your mother and father doted on you, naturally. And right after you started having those fainting spells your mother lost a baby. It was early on, oh goodness, you do know about babies and all. I am not telling you something new am I?"

Cassandra shook her head, "Of course, you know I am eleven years old." Satisfied, her grandmother continued. "Your parents bought the house your father lives in now and they hoped for more children, but then Camilla became very ill with a fever and she simply didn't recover, that's all. Tragic really, but no one grieved more than your father. The light seemed to leave his eyes when he lost her. I hoped that having you would eventually restore him to his old self, but he always carries that grief with him."

Cassandra nodded. This made sense because she always thought her father seemed sad, but she never knew exactly why. She thought it had something to do with her, but she liked her grandmother's explanation better.

"Now eat, or you won't have any energy for the rest of the afternoon." She did as her grandmother instructed. What an afternoon they had. Once back on Jenny, Leora took her to see the most beautiful waterfall she had ever seen and more paths that looked like places she would find the Menehune. As the sun began to set, they returned to the house and washed up for dinner. Cassandra sat on an overstuffed floral chair in the large room while Leora prepared supper and before she knew it, she was asleep.

14

For the next few weeks they followed the same pattern. Leora would pick her up after breakfast and they would set out to have an adventure. Leora taught Cassandra to ride Jenny and she would ride Charley Horse, a name that never failed to make Leora laugh when she said it. She also took Cassandra shopping for appropriate riding clothes in Honolulu. Everywhere they went people knew Leora and Cassandra could see that they enjoyed her as much as she did. She didn't see much of her father during this time. He often came home late after she had gone to bed and left in the morning before she arose. In that way, it felt like life in Maui and she didn't miss him.

She had decided not to tell Leora yet about the Menehune visit or her secret Gift, although she didn't know why. Maybe because her grandmother, so straightforward and no nonsense, wouldn't go for anything that sounded like a fantasy. Only a few days remained before the fall school term. Cassandra took her entrance exams and they placed her in the 5th grade exactly where she thought she belonged. She hadn't met any children and wondered how this whole school thing would work. Of course, she had read about schools and classrooms, but those books tended to be short on details about how one should behave in school. She wished she could ask someone, but it embarrassed her to admit her fear and anxiety about a simple thing like attending school.

Her school required a uniform, so Leora purchased them. On the first day, Cassandra dressed in the blue and green plaid cotton jumper with a white short-sleeved blouse, black shoes with white socks. It seemed strange to her to be dressed like this when she had spent most of the summer in pants. Leora drove her on the first morning of her school. She pulled up to the curb and waited for Cassandra to get out, but Cassandra bowed her head. "Leora, I am not certain if I should say a prayer or not. Mr. Mister began our lessons with prayer and he said if I am scared I should ask God to help me."

Leora made a little noise, "Don't worry now, you'll be fine. You should be your usual sweet self. You have good manners and you are a good listener so I am not worried about you. Now go on or you'll be late."

As she walked into the school, the unfamiliar scene overwhelmed her. Numbers of children of different ages, dressed alike in their uniforms, yet all so different. She asked a girl where she could find the 5th grade classroom, and the girl smiled and said, "Come with me, I'm going that way myself, come on." Cassandra found a desk with her name on it and sat down, following everyone else's lead. She read the teacher's name on the board. Miss Conrow. Tall, a youthful face with few wrinkles, the palest yellow hair, steel framed glasses and a sporty pale pink linen suit, which reminded her of candy. She didn't smile, but maintained a serious look as she watched the children settle into their desks.

They spent most of the morning listening to rules, many rules explaining what they should and shouldn't do. Miss Conrow instructed them to write them all down in their composition books so that they wouldn't forget them. Although there were many children, they were very quiet. At lunchtime, she could hear others marching to the cafeteria. She learned that morning that one of the most important rules was no talking in the hallways. The rule didn't apply in the cafeteria, and the noise there hurt Cassandra's ears, as unaccustomed as she was to children and their natural sounds.

That night, many thoughts rolled across her mind as she fought sleep. It shocked her to learn that unlike adults, where she had to concentrate to hear their thoughts, with children the opposite occurred and she couldn't find a shut-off valve. Halfway through lunch she realized that the noise didn't come from the children's mouths alone, but she heard their thoughts too. She noticed it in the classroom, but when the children concentrated on their work, it became quieter. That first day consisted mostly of shuffling about from place to place with lots of rules to remember. She didn't talk to anyone except the girl who led her to her class. Exhausted from this new experience she realized she needed to learn quickly how to shut The Gift off because she had already learned too much and feared someone might discover her. For example, she heard one boy's mean thought about how strange her hair looked. A girl saw her name on her desk and thought it sounded like it came from an old book. When Cassandra heard it, a tear came to her eye, which she tried to stop before anyone noticed. She must find a way to stop hearing their thoughts.

The next day seemed easier although she must have had a strange look on her face because in the cafeteria a teacher came over to her and asked her to follow her out into the hallway where she inquired if she felt ill. "No, ma'am. I am unused to being with so many children at once, and I suppose the noise is a bit overwhelming for me." Satisfied, the teacher sent her back to the table where her class sat having lunch.

Cassandra's mind spun with this new experience and found that she could fit in if she watched everyone else and followed along. She learned how to raise her hand, not speak out of turn, and how to play kick ball at recess. Sadly, she also found that most of the girls in her class already had friends and no one appeared to want a new one.

On Saturday, her father greeted her when she came down for breakfast. He put his paper aside and said, "Well? I expect a full report. How did you find your school, everything you expected?"

She decided not to tell him it felt as if she were invisible. No one spoke to her unless she asked a question. She survived that first week only because her class ate at an assigned lunch table, but no one paid any attention to her. When they had recess, the teacher organized them into kickball teams. Instead of the truth she said, "It is very interesting. I know that I asked to go to school, but I don't have any friends yet. Everyone else has known each other for a long time and I guess it's basically because I am new."

He frowned at the unnecessary information. "Actually I was inquiring about your classes. Were you adequately prepared to study at the fifth-grade level?" She shrugged because she didn't know how to answer him. She studied his thoughts instead, *Now what is wrong with her? Why won't she answer me?*

"Yes, Father, I do believe I am placed at the right level." There, that seemed to satisfy him and she hoped it signaled the end of his questions.

"That's fine then. By the way, your grandmother called to say she will pick you up this afternoon and then you may spend the night with her. How does that suit you?" She responded with an enthusiastic smile. "I see that news made you happy. Well, Mr. Takamura has fixed some of the special cake she likes; don't forget to take them with you."

"Yes, Father, don't worry, I won't forget." With that, she ran upstairs to get ready, glad to be out of his line of sight. She had made up her mind. Today she would talk to Leora about the friend situation and get her advice.

Later that evening, as they enjoyed their dinner she plunged into the subject. "Leora, you told me I could ask you anything."

"Well, yes I did, Cassie." After a few weeks, her grandmother had declared that Cassie was a more fitting name for her than Cassandra. "What's up? I'll bet it is about that new school and all."

"Yes, yes it is," she stammered, always surprised at how much her grandmother knew about her. "You see, no one actually talks to me, it's like I am invisible. I ask questions and the boys and girls are polite enough, but no one asks me anything or even bothers to sit by me. Please tell me Leora, is there something wrong with me?" Now that she had said it aloud and her words hung in the air Cassandra felt all of the emotion she had held inside well up in her throat. "I don't know what I expected, but I thought the other girls might like me a little and I might make a friend. But as I explained, it's like I'm not there at all."

Leora studied her face. "I'm pleased that you came to me Cassie, and that you trusted me with this. Now let's work at the problem from two sides shall we? You have told me already that no one has approached you, but what have you done at school to make friends?"

Cassie looked at her blankly. "Well, I don't know, I guess not much. The truth is I don't have any idea what I should do. I never read a book about it."

Leora smiled at that. "Are there any other girls in the class that are like you? Girls who aren't with a group or obviously more alone?"

Cassandra thought for a moment. "No, everyone has someone and other than the large group there are two other sets of girls, but how do I ask them?"

"What do you mean by that Cassie, how would you ask them what?"

Cassandra, embarrassed, put her head down. "You know, how do I ask them to be my friend?"

Leora sighed. "I apologize; I sometimes forget how much of life you missed on that hilltop. It doesn't exactly work like that, Cassie. You told me that everyone knows each other, right?" Cassie nodded.

"Then your job is to figure out which girl you might like for a friend. For example not all the girls are kind, correct? You are a very kind girl. There are certain things, activities you enjoy and not others, correct again?" As Cassie nodded again Leora shouted, "Yes again, of course I am right. Cassie girl, use this time when you feel alone to get to know the others. You can do that by simply observing. And, this is important, whenever anyone asks you to do something you make sure that you do it."

"Like what?" Cassandra was not quite following Leora's suggestion.

"Okay, like be on their team or walk with them somewhere, or sit next to them, anything. I can't believe no one asked you anything this first week of school. Well, all right then, are you willing to work at this?" Cassandra nodded. "Good girl, then I am going to give you an assignment. Next time we meet, I want you to tell me about at least five girls in your class. I want to know their names and everything you have learned about them, but also what you have in common with them. Do you think you can do that?" Cassandra nodded, now a little teary from the emotion she now felt. "Cassie," Leora took her chin in her hand, "You are learning about life now, do you understand? Before you were by yourself and you felt loneliness and now you are in a school crowded with children and you still feel alone. That is a great lesson, isn't it? Merely being around people doesn't automatically erase loneliness."

She reached out, took Cassie in her arms, and held her while she sobbed, glad to be able to release her feelings to someone who understood. "Enough." Leora suddenly declared, "let's get to bed, lots of work to do tomorrow and we need to get up before the sun." The next morning found Cassandra still sound asleep when Leora tickled her nose. "Good morning Mary Sunshine. Let's go for a ride." She gently pulled Cassandra up. "First we need to get the horses saddled, pack our lunch and get out the new seeds I want to plant on the upper ridge."

Now fully awake Cassandra said, "I can pack the lunches."

"Good girl, you do that while I get Jenny and Charley Horse ready. Don't forget your hat, last week your head got sunburned and I don't want that happening again." Cassandra felt very adult making their lunches and packing them in the old knapsack. She glanced around the old house, now so familiar to her. I don't want anything to change, not ever. I have never felt so much, before I only felt empty. She knew now why she felt different. Feeling something, even sadness, was better than no feeling at all. Amazingly, simply by sharing her true feelings with her grandmother made her heart feel lighter, unburdened. She could never imagine doing that with her Father. Ever.

15

She had dreamt lately of Pinao Ula and the Menehune, but her dreams weren't as clear as they used to be. In her dream, she felt the Pinao Ula calling to her, but she didn't go to him, as though her happiness prevented her from following. As they rode the horses up what she had once considered an extremely narrow path into the thick tropical foliage, she wondered what Nurse would think if she could see her now. Outside all day on a horse and sleeping like a rock, as Leora put it, at night. Yes, she felt content and suddenly had no reason to read anyone's thoughts, not when she felt as full as she did with these feelings inside her.

A few weeks later Cassandra awoke to the sound of heavy rain outside. She quickly got up and dressed. She knew Mr.Takamura would want to leave early because of the rain and the traffic. She had been working on Leora's assignment, watching and making mental notes about the girls in her class. Strangely enough, the task distracted her and she forgot about being an outsider or that she spent most of the time alone. Her classmates did speak about her and occasionally someone would speak directly to her. Her teacher paired them up and she often found herself partners with an abnormally shy boy named Leo who would barely grunt at her when they were working together. No matter how hard Cassandra tried to get him to talk, he remained almost mute. *Great,* she thought, *I finally have a chance to get to know someone and he is abnormally quiet.*

Then the notes began arriving, first one and then two more in her desk. Notes that said unkind things about her, her hair and her smell. She couldn't figure out why anyone would do this to her. In order for her to find out, she would have to do what she had promised herself she wouldn't; she would have to read thoughts again.

The next day, as they came in from recess she sat at her desk and slowly opened it. Yet another note stared back at her. Slowly she opened it with the desktop shielding it from any onlookers. It said,

> Do you notice how C_A_S_S_A_N_D_R_A
> (as if someone said it slowly)
> Thinks she's *better* than everyone else?
> What's wrong with CASSANDRA?

Cassandra took the note in her hand, held it tightly and began to look around the room. She paused briefly at each person to hear what he or she were thinking. At the same time, Miss Conrow asked them to get out their journals and write for five minutes, so Cassandra could conveniently record what she had heard. At the end of five minutes Cassandra had identified four girls who were thinking pretty much the same thing, *Did she see the note? Does she know who it is?* One of the girls said to herself, *Maybe we should stop this. It's too mean.* When she heard that she thought, there's my chance for a friend, and scribbled a note. She heard other interesting thoughts too, some sad and others just plain silly.

As she opened her math workbook, she purposely shut off The Gift. *I don't want to know any more* she thought. That night she began to devise a plan, one that would let them know they had made a mistake, and maybe she could make a friend in the process.

When Mr. Mister had told her about her aunt, Cassandra decided that she would only use The Gift for good, but now as she thought about how mean these girls were being to her for no reason she changed her mind. She decided that teaching them a lesson would be a good thing and considered the best way to do so. She carefully took old magazines Mr. Takamura had given her for a school mural and cut up letters for messages, a method she had read about in her mystery books. The next day she executed her plan; everyday she would place one note in one girl's desk and watch to see her reaction and hear her thoughts.

She thought for a long time about what she had learned about each girl and tailored each message to be particularly infuriating. For the first girl, Gayle, she put together this note:

> Gayle Gayle, fat as a pail,
> No one will ever like piggy old Gayle.

Being the first try, she wanted to hit the target. Everyone knew how sensitive Gayle felt about her weight, how upset she became if anyone mentioned it. After everyone left for lunch and recess, Cassandra ran back into the classroom and pretended to grab something from her desk. She turned to check behind her while she slipped the note out of her pocket and into Gayle's desk. She couldn't wait until after lunch and took her seat to watch. Gayle came into the classroom, opened her desk to get her journal and saw the note. Slowly, as if it were on fire she lifted it out of her desk, thought better of it and slipped it back into the desk. Cassandra could hear her think; *What is this? Is it a mistake? Did someone put Cassandra's note back into my desk?*

As far as Cassandra could tell, Gayle didn't look at the note all afternoon. At the end of the day she saw her put it into her pocket, still unread. Cassandra reconsidered her original plan to leave one note a day. As she came out of the school building, she noticed Gayle walking by herself with her head down and the other three weren't in sight. Maybe she would let it go a day and see what happened.

The next day things became more exciting as she saw Gayle, a little red-eyed, talking to the other girls at recess. She could see them pointing over at her and giving her looks as if somehow they knew. She decided she didn't care and didn't even try to read their thoughts for the rest of the day since she already knew what they thought.

Two days later, she decided it was time for another note. She put a note in Candy's desk and the magazine letters spelled out:

Her name may be Candy, but she isn't sweet,
I wish I could tell her I think she's a creep.

Now she knew Candy wouldn't cry because she operated as the boss of the group. She felt good putting the note into Candy's desk at recess.

The next morning as she sat down Candy came and stood next to her desk, and for the first time spoke directly to Cassandra. "So what do you think you are doing, *Cus-san-dra*?" She drew out the syllables slowly as if her name even sounded stupid.

"Why, just sitting here, what are you doing Candy?" She smiled and looked her straight in the eye.

"Did you leave a note in my desk?"

"Why would I do that, Candy?" She answered sweetly, but then she read her thoughts and they weren't pretty. In fact, Cassandra could safely predict that if she didn't stop the notes she would get a pounding.

"Oh, never mind," said Candy and she stomped back to her desk.

Over the weekend Cassandra decided the next chance she had, she would confess everything to Leora, including how she had vowed to stop using her Gift, but when she did it was worse than when they ignored her, because now they were angry with her. Saturday finally arrived and she put on her riding clothes and packed her overnight bag. With being at school all day and staying at Leora's most weekends, she now saw her father even less. She woke up early and made some notes for herself so she could practice sharing with Leora.

Her father laid his paper aside when she came into the dining room for breakfast. "I am afraid you are not going to your grandmother's today Cassandra. We have some work to do here and Doctor Fellows is going to pay you a visit."

Cassandra could feel her face reddening. "Why didn't you tell me before now?" She said this a little more crossly than she meant to, but she had a plan to execute.

Her father looked at her strangely. "Young lady, I don't think I have to ask permission to keep my own daughter at home now do I?"

"No, Father." She turned on her heel to go back upstairs when he called her back.

"Come on in here, sit down and have some breakfast. Tell me all about school. Here you have been back home all this time and I don't know a thing." She sighed and sank down in her place and waited for Mr. Takamura to bring her eggs and toast. She drank her juice obediently.

"I am waiting," her father said, "Tell me how things are progressing, especially your grades. Oh, and last time you mentioned friends, have you made any?" She looked at him and wondered is he truly interested? How strange after all this time he would ask me about school or friends.

She constructed her response carefully in her mind before she spoke. "Father, it is a new school for me and everyone else has been together for all five grades, so I expect it will take some time for me to be accepted. Don't get me wrong, no one is mean to me or anything like that. I mean, you know I am still an outsider." She quickly went on to the academic portion of her speech, "The school work it is very easy for me. Mr. Hunter must have been giving me all of the right lessons because I seem to get all top marks." There, she did it. Mission accomplished. She looked at her father innocently. "Now may I go?" He picked up his paper and said, "Go ahead."

16

Disappointed that she couldn't go to the plantation, as Leora called it, Cassandra toyed with politely asking if she could call Leora. She wanted to hear her big, happy voice, but she didn't want to cause trouble so she planned the day for herself. She began by writing down all of the things she wished to speak to her grandmother about, then all the possible responses Leora might have and she listed ideas about what to do next with the girls at school.

Next, she decided to write about what she wanted to do with her life. Her teacher had been talking about life goals, which sounded big and important, and she realized that she had never given it much thought. Whenever she read about an interesting city or a natural wonder she would think, someday I would like to go there. But her teacher had explained that's only a wish or a dream, and in order for a dream to become a reality you have to set goals.

She spent the rest of the morning creating her life goals and scribbling ideas about how she might be able to achieve them. She wrote of her desire to be like her Grandmother, to be an independent spirit, to support herself and to help others whenever she could. She thought that helping others might be her mission, but she couldn't quite be sure. Another goal was to go to college, although she had no idea what she would study. Finally, she wanted to travel and see the world. It occurred to her that she hadn't included a goal about having a family of her own, although she knew that was something she wanted, but way off in the distance.

Dr. Fellows's exam took much of the afternoon, uneventful other than his declaration that his visits would no longer be necessary. Apparently, over the past few months here in Honolulu, her heart had become stronger and he could barely hear the same sounds he had heard before. "In spite of what everyone thought," he said, "The warmer, damp air of Oahu has not harmed you at all; in fact it may have made you stronger." He even recommended that she take up some kind of sport, nothing too strenuous to start. Certainly nothing like tennis, but perhaps a sport like badminton, something she could learn with other children. He even thought swimming would be a good idea as she got older. Nothing too strenuous, he repeated, nothing competitive. Cassandra hugged him farewell, trying not to overdo the fact that he had at last confirmed what she felt all along – her heart had healed.

The next weekend Leora came to pick up Cassandra. When she heard the Jeep come up the drive, she impulsively ran down the stairs and out the front door. Cassandra had become quite good at telling the adults what they wanted to hear, and this worked especially well after she had read their thoughts and used the information to confirm what they wanted to hear. The results were astonishing and most of the time it achieved her desired outcome. Leora's thoughts were the only ones closed to her and today she intended to find out why. As Leora jumped out of the Jeep, Cassandra ran up to her, hugged her tightly and wouldn't let go. "I really missed you, and I have so much to tell you."

Leora laughed and hugged her back, "All right, now have you got your knapsack? Good girl. Today we are going up to Manoa Falls; there are things I would like to show you and lunch is all packed."

As they climbed into the Jeep, Cassandra became aware of how much it meant to have someone like Leora in her life, full of excitement and adventures that had she never imagined. In just a short time she had learned a great deal from her.

As they rode up to the trailhead, parked and grabbed their packs for the hike up to the falls Cassandra began her questioning. "Now Leora," she said quite seriously, "I really need to talk to you today about many things that have been bothering me, and before I begin I want you to know that I don't want you to worry about me, no matter what I tell you."

Leora winked at her, threw her pack on and held out her hand. "No promises, Cassie girl, no promises, but you might be surprised by just how much I already know."

As they began the hike they didn't talk much as the rocky and muddy trail required their concentration. At the falls they found a small clearing, threw their packs down and went for a quick swim in the pond at the bottom of the waterfall. Leora was always ready for a swim and had taught Cassandra that being ready to swim in Hawaii, no matter where you are, is an obligation. It is a gift one must graciously accept, part of the privilege of living here, Leora insisted. "In a few weeks Cassie girl, we will go to Waimea Falls again, does that sound good to you?" Leora asked her, although she knew the answer would be yes. As they settled down in the clearing to eat their lunch, now refreshed after their swim, Cassandra took the list of things to discuss with Leora out of her pocket and began studying it in earnest. Leora looked at her with surprise, "You have a list?"

Cassandra looked up, "Yes, I didn't want to forget a thing, and please let me get this all out before you say anything" and she began reading. "Grandmother, uh Leora, you know I didn't know anything about you when I lived in Maui and finding out about you began the first of many surprises. I don't know if anyone understood how much I missed having a mother, but for the first time in my life, I have someone who is like a mother to me. I know you met Nurse, but she is nothing like a mother, and Father only visited once a month. Father is also, what I would call formal – not mean-spirited– but well, just formal."

Cassandra looked up, took a deep breath and continued, "When I first learned that I had a grandmother I became angry. Yes, angry with you for not writing to me and angrier with my father for not telling me about you. I lived all alone in that little attic prison for five long years without anyone to really love me."

She looked up and saw Leora listening intently with a sweet look on her face. She quickly continued, "But when I met you, all of my anger seemed to melt away and now I can truly say that I am not angry anymore. I forgive you for not writing to me and I forgive Father for not telling me about you. There, I am finished." She wiped away a little tear, relieved of the emotion.

Leora asked, "May I tell you something now or do you want me to wait until you are completely done, because I believe there may be more." Cassandra nodded for her to continue.

Leora said, "I did write you at least once a week about everything happening here. I also wrote about your mother and my memories of her, as well as your grandfather. I shared the story of how we met, and our life together." Almost to herself she quietly added, "Even though he has been gone almost 20 years I still miss him. And I wrote you my story, about growing up and the planting the upper Nuuanu Valley. I wrote you about my dream that you would come back to Honolulu, how we would spend time together in my little shack, and about all the things I would teach you about the valley, the plants and riding. All these things I wrote to you, my dear Cassie, all these things.

Puzzled Cassandra asked, "But then why didn't I get any letters?"

"Oh," Leora looked sad now, "Your father and that stupid doctor felt that it wouldn't be good to fill your head full of silly dreams of coming home to Honolulu. That somehow it would only give you false hope. You see, my dear, I don't think they expected you to live very long. The first year, which you probably can't remember, your father spent most of the time in Maui with you, but then when you didn't die and you even seemed to improve somewhat he went back to work and only traveled to Maui occasionally. Anyway, I kept all of the letters and I have them for you, waiting for a time when you might show some interest or at least a bit of chutzpah and ask why I never wrote you." As she laughed at her joke, Cassandra ran to her and hugged her tightly.

They finished their lunch and Cassandra again picked up her paper and said, "Leora, I have a big secret and it has been difficult not to tell you about it before, but I have to now." She slowly relayed the story of the Menehunes' visit, the Dragon and The Gift. As Leora listened intently, she told her what Mr. Mister had shared about her aunt. She ended with how betrayed she felt by the adults in her life who would not trust her with the truth, but kept it hidden. She stopped with this accusation still on her lips, and looked at Leora, whose thoughts she never could read and asked, "Please tell me the truth, do you think that makes me a hateful girl?"

Leora laughed, "Hateful? Absolutely not. I think you have what I would call righteous indignation. You should be angry that no one ever thought to tell you about your aunt, but I should also tell you though, that your aunt's death caused your grandparents a lot of pain and most people want to bury their pain. Now wait a minute, let's back up here a second. If you can read others' thoughts as now you know your aunt could, how come you never read my mind?"

"Well, it is the strangest thing. I can't. I have tried many times, but I never can. It is like there's a wall and I can't see through it."

Again, Leora threw her head back and laughed. "That isn't much of a trick, Cassie old girl. It is merely something I learned to do as a girl when I became aware that others could read my thoughts and might use them against me. You see, it didn't used to be so unusual to have the ability to read another person's thoughts, but as your minister told you, most people thought of it as the work of evil spirits and didn't want anything to do with it. I practiced blocking others from reading my thoughts and I guess I got used to it and never turned it back on again." She smiled at that. "It isn't much of a trick after all. Most people could do what you have done if they are open to the idea and truly focused on the other person, just as you have. It should also not surprise you that there is a way to protect others from reading your thoughts as I have discovered. Does that make sense?"

"I guess so," Cassandra said. Looking at her paper only one subject remained and she thought, *I wonder when I should tell her about the girls and the notes, I don't want her to be disappointed in me.*

"Well," said Leora as she packed up the lunch remains and got ready to leave, "Have you talked about everything you wanted to discuss today?" When Cassandra didn't answer immediately, Leora asked, "All right, then how are things going with the school and friends and about that plan we talked about last time?"

Cassandra sighed, sat down, told her the entire sordid story, including how bad she felt when she saw her words made Gayle cry and how she promised herself that she wouldn't write any more notes.

Leora said, "Good girl, glad to hear it. Now we need to work on Phase Two. Ask one of the girls to do something. Whatever you think might be fun for the two of you to do."

The suggestion horrified Cassandra. Until now she had only watched, waited and noted her observations. True, she knew a lot about each girl, but the thought of asking one to do something with her shook her to the core. After school, she would talk to Mr. Takamura as he fixed dinner or give Nurse some tidbits that would satisfy her curiosity about what happened at school. She couldn't imagine doing either of those things with someone else.

Leora said, "It doesn't have to be a major event you know. You have been watching them for a few weeks now; you must have an idea what they do after school or on weekends don't you?"

She thought for a minute. She knew that Diane lived relatively close and that sometimes Diane walked while she rode. "That's it," Cassandra said. "I will ask Diane if she wants to come home with me after school with Mr. T. and then we could take her home."

"Or," Leora said, "If she walks home, why don't you walk with her?"

"That's true, if Father would allow me to walk home from school."

"Goodness Cassie, don't be a silly girl, of course he will. Simply tell Mr. T. that you are walking with a friend. So then, it's a plan? Next week I expect to hear how it goes." She handed her a piece of paper. "You know, I do own a telephone. I know you were disappointed last weekend when you couldn't come over, but in the future if you ever want to talk to me just call me up." They quickly packed up and hiked back to the Jeep, aware that the clouds were telling them the afternoon showers would soon begin.

Cassandra lay in bed that night thinking of everything she and Leora had discussed, once again fighting sleep so that she could review everything she had learned and think further on her new plan for school. Smiling to herself as she imagined how pleased Leora would be with all of her ideas and plans, she finally drifted off to sleep.

17

On Monday, Miss Conrow asked for their attention as soon as they settled into their desks. A tall, slender boy with shiny chestnut-brown hair and light colored eyes stood in front of the room looking very unhappy. Cassandra couldn't stop herself – she read his thoughts. Not a surprise, he felt nervous and didn't want to be there in front of everyone. *I don't want to stand up in front of everyone as the stupid "new kid". They are all staring at me like I am a monkey in the zoo.*

Miss Conrow explained that Zachery had recently moved from the mainland, not from California like many others, but from New York City. Cassandra, interested in the mainland as she planned to study there one day, hoped she could learn from him. When Miss Conrow asked him to tell the class something about himself, he mumbled, "No thanks" and sat down in his front row seat.

It occurred to Cassandra that this boy's arrival offered her a chance to be viewed differently as she would no longer be the newest kid in class, and no longer the only outsider. However, Zach seemed to get on better than she had. Because of his natural athletic ability, all the boys wanted him on their team. He demonstrated what their teacher called good sportsmanship and soon friends weren't a problem for him. By the end of that first week, it seemed as if he had been there forever, which only made Cassandra feel more ill at ease about her friend-less status.

On Thursday she finally asked Diane – only because she knew her grandmother would expect a report – to walk home with her on Friday. Diane had a long face, which her long hair made even longer. Cassandra called her name as everyone exited for lunch so that they would be alone when she asked her. Diane looked at her curiously and then said, "I have to ask my mother and I'll let you know tomorrow." Then she ran off toward the other girls without even a look back at Cassandra. Cassandra wondered why she hadn't been quick enough to read her thoughts so now she had no idea if Diane would even consider it. Sighing, she slowly made her way out the door.

That night she lay in her bed trying to sleep and thought about why she so desperately wanted a friend. She thought, *I am being silly here. I don't need any more friends because who could ask for a better friend than Leora.* The thought comforted her and allowed her to sleep.

She waited the next morning for Diane to come into the back of the classroom where many of the children hung their school bags. She finally saw her, taking every ounce of courage to smile and wave hello to her. "What did your mother say; can you walk home with me this afternoon?"

Diane looked down at her feet. "Oh, sorry. I forgot to ask her." She pushed past Cassandra and went to her seat.

As Cassandra walked to her seat she thought, *now I'm sorry I didn't use the poem I had for her note.* Soon it would be the holidays and Leora had promised to take her to the Big Island to see the volcano and visit with some of her cousins in Hilo. Although Cassandra's life differed dramatically from what it had been just a few months ago, she felt the need for a change. She now realized that she and her father had little to talk about and she further noted that as long as she remained physically well and didn't bother him, everything went smoothly.

Then a month before the Christmas break the unimaginable happened. Her father called her into his study when she came in from school. She had rarely been in his study, because she usually interacted with him in the dining room.

"Please, sit down." His voice sounded unusually kind, and as she looked at him across the large teak desk, she had a sinking feeling. Her first thought was that they would have to leave Honolulu for some reason.

"Cassandra, I don't quite know how to say this to you, but I know you are a big girl now and not a baby so I am going to tell you straight out. Your grandmother died this morning. She went for an early morning ride, and something must have happened. They found her on the trail. Probably a stroke or heart attack. We'll never know, but when you are eighty years old these things can just happen."

Cassandra, stunned beyond words or thoughts, just stared at him, trying to make sense of his words. She tried to form a response, tried to think of something to say, but she couldn't. She jumped up and ran upstairs to her room, anxious to be alone and away from everyone. She lay face-down on her bed, feeling, finally feeling the pain, as loud sobs rose up in her throat. How unfair, how could this happen? She finally has someone in her life that cares for her, with whom she could share her secrets and suddenly she is gone.

When she woke up she lay in bed in her pajamas; probably Nurse had come over. She didn't know how long she had slept, but as soon as she remembered what had happened she starting sobbing, feeling as though her heart had broken. She thought, *I never want to get up,* and then she cried herself back to sleep.

There would be no funeral as her grandmother had specifically forbade it; the body would be cremated and her ashes spread in the Nuuanu Valley. Her father told her all of this with no emotion as he sat across from her while she lay in bed. He had been kind the last few days with her, but she could see him becoming increasingly impatient with every discussion.

"Today," he announced, "You will get up and get ready for school. Breakfast will be ready downstairs and I myself will drive you."

Again, she thought, no one in this family ever talks about what has happened. She glared at him and demanded, "Why can't we ever talk about things?"

Her father looked shocked and stopped in his tracks, "What do you mean?"

"You know I could tell Leora anything and she would tell me anything I asked of her. Why can't you be like that?" Her father looked down. "I don't want to go to school anymore. I want to stay in my room."

"Cassandra," her father finally said slowly and carefully, "People die, it is part of life. You don't remember when your mother died, but I do and eventually the pain will lessen and you will be able to go on with your life. In the meantime you cannot lie in bed."

She stared at him again. "No, this pain will never go away. I can't explain it to you, you would never understand, but I am not going to school."

Her father moved toward her now, clearly agitated. "I have tried to be patient with you, but I am out of patience. Your grandmother would have been ashamed to see you carry on like this. I know that I will never be able to take your grandmother's place, but I would at least expect you to give me a chance. When I come back into the room, I expect to see you dressed and ready for school." He strode out of the room and shut the door firmly.

Hot tears rolled down Cassandra's face. When her father had said Leora would be ashamed of her, it cut her straight to the heart and she felt unbearable pain. To never see Leora again, never hear her laugh or hug her seemed the worst punishment in the world. Cassandra slowly sat up and determined that once she was old enough to leave home she would never return and furthermore she would never forgive her father for not understanding what she had lost so soon after finding it.

She went to school and she did her work until the Christmas break, but she felt empty and dead inside as if she were simply going through the motions. Then on a January morning before school, her father again called her into his study. "Cassandra," he said, "Come in here. I have something for you." Her father stood next to his desk with a beautiful large red leather box. "Your grandmother had some things she wanted you to have, letters and a number of pictures. We can talk about the house and the rest later, but right now you should know she left these for you."

"Father, what about her house? What will happen to the horses and the stables and everything that is in the house?" Cassandra could feel her voice becoming strident with emotion.

"Please sit down." Her father said and looked at her directly. "Your grandmother left everything she had in the world to you; however, since you are a minor I will serve as the trustee until such time as you are able to take over the estate yourself. Do you understand what that means?" She shook her head no. "It means I will make all of the decisions about the property and the money. Frankly, this is a great gift for you. It means once the horses, house and car are sold you won't have to worry about money for college or for some time after that."

"No. You can't sell the horses and house. We went riding together and...." Cassandra said rather loudly, especially for her. Her father appeared startled that she actually voiced an opinion or wanted to make herself heard.

"Cassandra," her father interrupted her, "The horses have already gone to a very good farm. Horses cost a great deal of money to house and feed and it would drain the estate. The house won't bring much, but the real value is the land around the house. It includes at least four hundred acres of prime real estate and that will amount to a great deal of money, provided it is sold at the right time."

"Father," now she calculated her thoughts and words. "I know you said that Leora willed the estate to me, correct?"

"Yes," he said, "That is true."

"Then shouldn't you at least discuss with me what is to be done?" Now tears were coming without her stopping them.

"Cassandra, you must understand that taxes will be due on the property and we don't have the money to pay for them. There is some cash as part of the estate, but using it to maintain the property will leave less for your future."

"I want to understand, I do. I can understand why the horses were sold because I can't take care of them and I am glad they are going to a good home. But, I absolutely want to keep Leora's house and land because someday I want to live there. Of course," she added quickly, "When I come back from college." She thought that would pacify him, but she could see it only annoyed him.

"I'm happy you are taking an interest in your future and I expected you to have a passion for your grandmother's estate, however as I told you, I am the trustee and I am the only who will make the decisions. I promise you that I will take your wishes into consideration, but I have to do what is best for the estate and for you long term."

"When will the estate be turned over to me?"

"When you are 21, my dear."

"Father," she began, but as she started to launch another argument she saw that he had concluded the interview.

"That's all for now. Again, here is the box of mementos your Grandmother left. I can promise you one thing, in deference to your Grandmother's wishes I will make no further decisions without talking to you first. However, you must understand that ultimately I will be the one making the decisions."

"Yes, Father, thank you." she said, slowly taking the box and climbing upstairs to her room.

The great sadness that had descended upon her when she had heard of Leora's death did not go away. There were days when she was convinced it never would. She treasured the letters and it turned out exactly as Leora had promised, at least one letter for every month she had been on Maui. They were beautiful descriptive letters and as she read them she could almost hear Leora's voice reading them to her. She read one a day until she had read them all and then she started all over again. As she heard Leora's voice speaking to her through the letters Cassandra's heart began to heal.

18

School started to get better for one reason. At long last she had made a friend. It had simply happened and now she understood that finding friends must happen exactly like that. One day at recess she sat by herself, hoping someone would ask her to play as they sometimes did, especially when they needed to even out the teams. On this day no one had had invited her, so she sat off to one side of the playground on a wooden bench reading her book. She felt someone sit down next to her, but she didn't think anything of it and didn't bother to look up.

"Hey you," the someone said. Now she looked up, extremely surprised that someone spoke to her and even more surprised to see Zack, the new boy, sitting there. She thought he should have had the title of the "last new kid in class."

"Hey yourself" she said as nonchalantly as she could, and then deliberately looked back at her book.

"Can I ask you something?" he said inching closer to her. She nodded, but kept her eyes glued to the page, not reading anything at all. "Is it true what they say about you?"

Her suspicions raised, she concluded that his motives couldn't be pure. She did not look up. "I don't know, what do they say about me?"

"That you are some kind of a weirdo; that you lived all by yourself up in the hills of Maui and you have some kind of disease." She lifted her head now and looked at him, and then she stood up to leave. She saw a look of innocence on his face. "Hey, wait a minute, I didn't mean to make you mad or anything. It's just that I got tired of hearing it from these guys and I wanted to talk to you myself. Come on, don't be angry." He followed her as she walked back to the classroom because the bell had rung, and she didn't want to hear anymore. "Listen." he had caught up with her. "I think you live near me. Would it be okay if I walked home with you from school some time?"

She turned to him, her face flush with embarrassment. "You mean you would be seen with me? A weirdo? Why would you want to do that?" She turned away from him, walked back into the classroom, and tried to stop herself from reading his thoughts.

After school, Zack was waiting for her as she came out of the building. She had told Mr. Takamura not to pick her up today, as she would be walking. She had hoped that Diane would have seen the light and would be walking with her. She didn't mind walking with Zack, but not because of some curiosity he had about her being a weirdo. As she began walking, she knew he followed behind her at an even pace. After a block she turned back, shouting over her shoulder at him, "Hey where do you live?"

"Up in Manoa Heights, same as you." He ran up beside her.

"Then how come I have never seen you walking home before?"

"Yesterday I had softball practice and before that I went to the YMCA or the library. This is the first week I am walking on my own."

"Oh. You can walk with me if you want to, then."

He laughed, "Well, okay then, thanks for the invite." So she had a friend. It turned out they liked the same kind of books, he liked to write and they talked easily with one another. Given his immediate popularity and affinity for sports, finding out they had common interests surprised her. Zack also wanted to learn about the islands and she became the one to tell him about it, having lived her entire life in Hawaii.

Soon everyone treated her as if she belonged and she felt better than she had, all because Zack had made her his friend. It astonished her, because she knew that he hadn't announced to anyone, "Hey, Cassie and I are friends everyone, she's okay." But she also knew that they had seen them talk and walk together. She resisted the temptation to read their thoughts and eventually concluded that they figured if Zack likes Cassie then they should, too. She couldn't get over how things had changed.

Soon it felt as if she had known Zack all her life. They spent most of their free time together doing homework, reading books and when she thought no one was looking, racing him home from school. She hadn't fainted since being back on Oahu and she believed what Dr. Fellows had said, that her heart had healed.

Zack played softball for spring sports with Cassandra as a regular fixture at his games, sitting with the same girls who had so rudely ignored her when she first arrived. None of it mattered as she watched Zack play, cheering him on. She finally felt herself feeling lighter and not missing Leora as much, although her absence left a different kind of hole in her heart.

After school let out that summer, her father took her up into the valley. They parked at Leora's house. Her father took the cylinder of ashes out of the car. "Where do you think we should spread these?" he asked.

"Follow me, I know just the place." When he told her what they were going to do, she had informed him that he should dress comfortably and wear walking shoes if he had any. Naturally, he had some, he said. Cassandra had just never seen them.

As they walked on the horse path away from the house she felt her eyes tearing up in spite of her best efforts to stop them. "This way Father, this is the way we would take the horses. It will take us a little longer on foot to get there but you'll see how beautiful it is." Confidently she led the way up onto the ridge and over to the bamboo forest. "Did you know that Leora and her grandmother planted this entire area?" she asked.

"No," he shook his head and his eyes were wide. "I have never been up here Cassandra, it is splendid beyond words." Together, they spread the ashes all across the large bamboo forest. It began to rain, not a downpour, just the light rain the valley usually received this time of the afternoon while the sun was still out. As they walked back to the car she asked, "Father, shouldn't we say a prayer or some words or something to remember her?"

He looked down as he walked, careful not to trip over the large roots in the path. "I don't know," her father sighed. "You know I haven't been much of a church-going man and neither was your grandmother. I guess we could ask the forest to take her back, you know ashes to ashes and dust to dust, that kind of thing."

She frowned and thought that's not exactly what I meant. She now realized that she had better get to know her father because he was all she had in the world. Leora's letters had showed a different side of him and as much as she trusted her grandmother, she wasn't ready to believe what she had read about him. "Cassandra?" her father called her back as she had become lost in her own thoughts.

She turned to him now, "It's just that there's a lot I didn't know about Leora and now that she is gone a part of me seems like it is missing. I knew her age and that she would die someday, but I didn't think it would so soon after I finally got to know her. I keep wondering why I only had such a short time with her."

Her father came closer to her and took her by the shoulders. "Now you understand what it is like to love someone and have to suddenly say goodbye to them. We don't always have the chance to say goodbye in the way we wish. That's why. . ." He stopped and looked away from her, "That's why I should have learned my lesson when your mother died." He walked away from her.

He now had Cassandra's undivided attention because he had never spoken to her as an adult, as an equal. "What do you mean?"

"My lesson. . ." he began as he continued walking down the narrow path that led to the back of the house. He looked out at the ocean. "The lesson I should have learned is that you must love people while they are alive, while they are in front of you, otherwise you end up doing what I did and what I am sorry for…."

She had followed him and now they were at the bottom of the path and they turned toward the house. "What could you be sorry for? Please tell me." She now thought she knew, but wouldn't say it for him, and she promised herself she wouldn't cheat by reading his thoughts.

"Come sit down in front of the house with me Cassandra." Together they sat in the old wooden chairs that overlooked the bluff and then out over the ocean. "I am sorry that when your mother died I shut myself off from the world. It all came back to me when your grandmother died and I saw how you reacted. We can't love just a memory. We have to love those in front of us or we only end up loving our memories. I thought that would be enough at first, but I found out it isn't. I found out that if you refuse to treat your memories only as memories you won't be able to love anyone else, it's not possible."

"It's not?" She asked her eyes wide with amazement.

"No, it's not, Cassandra." Now he turned to look at her with tears in his eyes. "I am so sorry for shutting you out all of these years. Since Leora died, I have realized what I have done to you and how much I have lost, how much time and how much love. Please, my darling daughter, please forgive me." He put his head in his hands and sobbed. Cassandra rose, went over to him and awkwardly wrapped her arms around him.

At that moment time didn't move for Cassandra, and nothing else seemed to matter. If her grandmother's death had caused this change in her life it must be for a good reason, and she felt that she had not lost Leora, because, after all, she had the letters. She hoped to have a real relationship with her father, not just an arrangement, which was how she thought of it. A simple arrangement with a father and daughter, living together only because of biology with no familial bond between them.

Cassandra, exhausted with the emotion of the day, helped her father pack up. As they drove back to the house in Manoa she began to drift off and as soon as they arrived she went to her room and slept through the night. Her dreams were full of color, light, and a little green-gold dragon, but her heart felt full of love and hope for what was to come.

19

7 years later

C assie stood in her room packing for college on the mainland. Her heart raced with excitement, only two days to go. She had never been on a plane and never had been to the mainland, and she didn't think she would sleep until then. The phone rang in the hallway and Mr. T, who moved a little slower these days, called up to her, "Cassie, Zack on the phone for you."

"Be right there." she yelled to him as she flew out to the hallway to pick up the phone. "Hey you. What's going on?"

Zack said, "Why are you out of breath?"

"Oh, you know, just excited about leaving that's all."

"Do you want to go to the beach this afternoon? Some of the gang are getting together up on the north shore and later we can get dinner. Okay?"

"Sure, see you in a bit." Although she and Zack had been close friends since the sixth grade, they weren't actually a couple, but everyone expected that wherever Zack went Cassie went too. They had graduated from high school a few months earlier and while Zack planned to study oceanography at the University of Hawaii, Cassandra had her heart set on going to the mainland to the University of Chicago. Leora's estate had made it possible for her to go anywhere she chose, and she spent months looking at schools, conducting her own serious research. Chicago, with its history and museums and great lake setting, sounded thrilling to her and an opportunity for the adventure she craved.

She had a nagging little feeling in the pit of her stomach, which began right after graduation; in fact, she knew exactly when it had happened. She and Zack had been at the beach surfing for the entire day. As they climbed into Zack's van to begin the drive home she suddenly felt very sleepy and she leaned against him, and told him how perfect the day had been. He turned suddenly and kissed her passionately. Shocked, she had snapped back and said something stupid like, "Zack what are you doing?" Red-faced, he had mumbled something and pulled out of the parking lot.

It was the first moment in all the years she had known him that he ever tried to kiss her and she felt like an idiot for responding the way she did. They had agreed freshman year that rather than go alone to dances or games that they would go together. Cassie didn't date at all during high school. She thought because they were inseparable it was no surprise that everyone assumed they were a couple. They were even on prom court together. Cassie looked out her bedroom window and thought, I like the way things have always been and I don't want them to change. Why did he have to do that?

She knew that the possibility of a more passionate relationship hung in the air between them, and had been ever since that day in the car. And having something unsaid between them was unusual. They had talked about everything from the time they first became friends, back in the fifth grade. She shared all of her concerns about the girls, teachers and her father and he did the same. Now that she thought about it how strange that neither one of them had broached the subject yet. She stood up in her room, determined that today would be the day. As Zack pulled up in front of the house and honked the horn, she readied herself to begin.

"We need to talk," she said as he pulled out of her driveway, "And we have lots of time to do it before we join the others."

"Fire away, Cassie girl," he said as if nothing had changed. He looked very much the part of the surfer boy today, as he had spent every day since graduation at the beach. His dark hair had even gained some highlights, bleached from the sun. His skin, always tan, now had turned the color of toast and she noted he had on her favorite dark green swim trunks splashed with white hibiscus. He looked particularly great today and she wondered what was wrong with her. She sighed and plunged ahead. "Okay you know we always share everything, right?" Zack nodded, "Well," she continued, "I have been thinking about what happened a couple of months ago and I thought it was just weird that we never talked about it, I mean really weird."

Zack frowned and looked ahead at the road, "Don't have any idea what you are talking about Big C, what happened a couple of months ago?"

"All right, come on, Zackaroo." Since he used the name he called her when they were younger, so did she. "Don't try to be funny, you know what I am talking about, that afternoon when I fell asleep and you kissed me."

"Hey, listen lady, I made a mistake, you know, too much sun, lightheaded and all." He laughed, but it didn't sound real to her.

"Zack, you and I have always told each other everything and we haven't been so good at it the last few months. I mean we talked about my going to the mainland and you said you would be able to get by, but what does that really mean? Aren't you going to miss me at all?" As the words came out of her mouth she felt stupid about even bringing this up now, and what did that have to do with him kissing her? She thought about a recent conversation with two girlfriends who were quizzing her about whether she and Zack would announce their engagement before she left for the mainland. Aloud she said, "Listen to me. I think we should talk about this, since we never have and I think we should be clear."

"What are you talking about?" now Zack looked genuinely worried. "Are you asking me what the 'status' of our relationship is? Because now you are starting to sound like my parents, who are always questioning me about us."

Ah, ha, she thought, that is new information. She smiled to herself. "I have never thought of us having a 'status.' I just thought of us as Zack and Cassie, best friends to the end. We always have so much fun together and we know each other so well, but now this pressure everyone is putting on us is coming between us."

"Everyone?" Zack asked. She replied,

"Zack, this is not news and you know it. Honestly, all through high school people would ask if we were going steady, did we plan to get married, but I ignored them. I didn't care what they thought because we were best friends and that was all that mattered to me. And I don't have to remind you; I never had any friends before you." Now Zack pulled over into a favorite spot of theirs just past Diamond Head. He parked the car and turned to look at her.

"Cassie, I know you don't remember this but a long time ago, I don't know, maybe in seventh grade, some of the guys were teasing me about you and you overheard them. I saw the look on your face and you looked like a bunny who wanted to bolt. I decided at that moment that I would be your friend first, before any other kind of relationship. I have never told you this before, but sometimes it is very difficult for me to be your friend." He looked at her with such a serious face that her heart began to pound.

"What do you mean by that?" she asked, hoping that he meant it in the way she thought.

"Ah Cass, you know this isn't a good time to have this conversation with you leaving and all. It will only complicate things. I meant what I said; I am your friend first." He turned away from her and looked out at the ocean.

"Okay Zack, then let me ask you a question that's been on my mind. Are you planning to date at U of H, and how do you feel about my dating when I am at college. Well?"

He sat quietly and continued looking out at the water. She felt her face getting hotter and hotter. Maybe the apple didn't fall far from the tree and like her father; she had avoided this entire subject for years. "Zack," she said quietly, "Are we just friends?"

Zack turned back to her and he looked angry now. "You don't understand at all, Cass." He got out of the car and walked down the beach to the water.

She sat there, stunned. All this time it had never occurred to her and she felt stupid for not seeing it sooner. He had no interest in her as a girl at all, just as a friend. She felt tears coming into her eyes and she thought, *what did I expect?* She couldn't believe it had never occurred to her before; that things wouldn't always continue as they had. She had always assumed they would always be together. She had no one, no one else in her life like him. That was the burning question; what would happen when they were apart?

She got out of the car and ran after him down onto the beach. "Zack. Zack." But he kept walking until finally she caught up with him. "Zack, please slow down, I need to talk to you. I never thought much about any of this, really I didn't. I was happy with us just being friends."

Zack stopped and plopped down in the sand looking at the water and the never-ending horizon ahead of him. "Okay, then Cass, sit down. I think you are right, we do need to talk and it might take a while. Don't worry, everyone will wait for us."

"Good" she replied, still a bit out of breath from running after him.

Zack swallowed hard, "Cass, this is hard for me to say, so let me take my time. When we first became friends, back in the summer between fifth and sixth grade, that's when we started doing everything together, do you remember? She nodded, of course she did. "Starting around seventh grade I started assuming things." He paused and took a deep breath. "I kind of assumed that we would date in high school and after college we would get married and have a home and we'd always be together. A fantasy, I guess. Remember when we were at that party at Jen's when we were in the seventh grade and I kissed you?"

"Yes, but that didn't count; we were playing a silly kids' game." She smiled now at his worried face.

"Yeah, I know," he said, "But ever since then I had kind of imagined how it would be to kiss you and hold you, and I mean more than just a hug or when you are crying like I have done in the past. I mean really hold you. But then as high school started and for a while there, during freshman year, you liked this guy, what his name?"

"Jon." she added.

"Oh yeah, Jon. He liked you too, and you were together in homeroom and English class and you wouldn't shut up about him, so I prepared myself, you know in case we were never going to be anything but friends. After a while, I decided that I would be okay with that. I never knew anyone like you and I love being with you. What we have is special and I never wanted to do anything that would mess that up." He stopped and Cassie thought for a minute.

133

"Okay, Zack and you know I feel the same way about you, but this is 1958 after all. A lot of kids our age are doing more than simple hand-holding; why do you think we never even felt the urge to do so?"

Zack had his head down, looking at the sand and he shook his head, "I don't know. Maybe I shouldn't tell you this, but do you remember when I went to San Diego to see my grandparents two summers ago?" She sure did, a rotten summer as far as she was concerned.

"Well, I stayed there for over a month and I met this girl, Tessie. She and her parents went to the same church as my grandparents. They knew each other really well, and we ended up spending a lot of time together. I took her out a couple of times and well, I would call her uh, aggressive, if you know what I mean. We were kissing and she always wanted more, but..." Now tears were trickling down Zack's face . . . And I just couldn't do it, I had no interest in her."

"So, what happened?"

"Nothing, except she got really mad at me and wouldn't talk to me for the rest of the time. She said some terrible things to me Cassie, that's partly why I never told you even though we usually tell each other everything."

"I don't get it, what terrible things did she say to you?"

Now his tears were flowing freely. "She said the reason I never did more than kiss her, well she said I liked boys more than girls. I got mad too, and said some pretty awful things to her about girls who fool around with someone they are not even serious about, and well, you get the picture."

He wiped his eyes and stood up. "Now that I finally have told you I feel better, come on we better get up to Haleiwa before everyone eats without us and then we have to get our own lunch."

"What? I don't care." Cassie said, still sitting in the sand. "I am not going until we finish this, and we can stop at one of the shrimp trucks on the way. Please sit here with me."

Zack sat back down and gently she put her arms around him. The two of them sat there for a long time with Cassie's slender arms around him. Finally in a small voice Zack said, "Do you think it's true? I never told you because I didn't want to know if you thought the same things about me, and I never wanted anything to change what we have."

Cassie sat back and said, "Now it's my turn Zack, listen to me. My life changed when we first became friends, remember? I became a different person with you. You were cool and popular, everyone liked you, and the fact that you were my friend opened up completely new worlds for me, remember?"

"Sure do."

"I dreamed about us being married too. It probably started in the seventh grade and I had that dream for a long time, even when we were in high school. Because you are my soulmate. Anyway, that's how I would describe you in my journals. I never worried about not having a physical relationship. Okay, I would wonder sometimes when I read about boys and listened to the other girls talk about their dates. They would go into detail about their boyfriend's physical demands and, well I just figured you were different. I believed you were better than they were, and finally I simply stopped worrying about it. Because, Zack," and she looked right into his clear blue eyes, "Because no matter what happens over the next four years nothing can change the bond we have between us, nothing as far as I am concerned." Then she leaned in and kissed him on the cheek.

"So," Zack sighed and put his arm around her, "Are you okay if we keep on the way we always have been for the summer and then try to figure this out later?"

"Absolutely," she said "But I want you to promise me something Zack." "What's that?" he said standing up and pulling her to her feet. "That if you ever become interested in someone else that you will tell me. Don't let me hear it from someone else, and for sure I don't want to hear about it in a letter."

"You got it, I promise." he said and they raced to the car.

They drove up to the north shore and joined their friends for late afternoon surfing. They lay on the beach as the sun started to set and the trade winds brought cooler air. She snuggled up to him in front of the fire they had built, and whispered, "See? As always, this is the best place of all for me." He put his arm around her and whispered back, "Soulmate."

20

T he rest of the summer flew and because her father had to be in court, Zack volunteered to drive her to the airport. She made it a point to come down and have breakfast with her father on her last morning at home. He seemed distracted as he always did when he had a trial beginning, and tried his best to go through some last-minute items with her but he couldn't help himself.

She finally said, "Father, listen, I am fine. If I need anything I will write or call or worst case send a telegram for bail money, okay?" He smiled at her. "I know and hopefully I will be in Chicago for Christmas and we can stay at the Drake just like your mother and I did many years ago, and we'll see the sights together. Promise me you'll have everything in hand by then."

"Of course, I'm looking forward to it. Now get your briefcase and get going or you'll be late."

Delighted to have the rest of the morning to herself to say goodbye to the house, she planned to visit each room. When she had first returned she often felt like an outsider or a guest, but now it felt more like home. She had driven out to Leora's place yesterday and spent the day there going through pictures and other mementos, trying to determine what she would ultimately have to give up. Her father had been true to his word and hadn't sold the place after all, but he told her that over the next year he would finally sell the Maui house. The sale would bring in a great deal of money and would allow him to relax a little and not work so hard. She told him he could sell anything except Leora's place because she planned to live in it one day. Much to her surprise, he agreed. At one point, a local developer offered them a large sum of money for part of the parcel to develop into high-end homes. Cassie had told her father "Absolutely not, none of it will ever be sold. Leora and her own grandmother planted most of it and someday I am going to finish her catalog of the area's flora and fauna."

"All right, Cassie, all right, we won't entertain any more offers on the property." Her father had eventually ended up calling her Cassie and their relationship had significantly improved since Leora had died, although she thought it had something to do with Zack.

When Zack began coming around regularly, often having dinner with them and then staying to study with Cassie, her father took a real interest in him. Zack and her father talked about oceanography at length, something that surprised Cassie. She had no idea of her father's interests, although she mused later, if she had paid attention she might have noticed the books he owned. They also both loved to play her father's favorite game, backgammon.

Sighing as she thought of the past, Cassie continued her sweep through the downstairs of the house, trying to memorize everything. She noted the few pictures her father had on the mantel and the large portrait of her mother, which hung over the fireplace. Cassie stared at her and thought, *I sure don't look much like her*. Camilla had long brown hair curled tightly with highlights of gold, which added a strange light to the picture. Cassie thought of it as an old-fashioned face, sweet and innocent, her skin portrayed as very pale, almost translucent.

Cassie had short hair since the fifth grade, which she wore on her head like a curly cap. While she would describe the color of her mother's hair as beautiful, hers was a dull dark brown with a little red that appeared when she spent time in the sun. She guessed it might have been similar to the kind of hair her father had before he had lost most of it.

She continued her tour, trying to remember everything, in case her father made good on his promise of doing whatever he wanted to with the Manoa home. She chided herself silently for thinking negatively about her father. Her grandmother's letters had put any mystery to rest. His sullen and serious demeanor and his formal style had been a mystery to her for most of her life, but now she understood him better.

Leora had written about her father, describing the man who first courted her daughter. Camille had studied in the states and when she returned to Honolulu, she had no plans to stay. When she fell in love with Andrew things changed. He refused to leave Hawaii, the war began, they married, and a year later had a baby. Her father blamed himself for Camille's unhappiness, her sickness and death, and he never forgave himself for keeping her in Hawaii.

Cassie didn't want to think about that now. It may be selfish, she thought, but this was her turn to live. Her chance to be on her own, to go to Chicago and be an adult, and not always live in her father's shadow. She believed the Menehune had told her to go and discover her life. She knew if she stayed in Honolulu everyone would expect her to get married to Zack and right now she couldn't envision that. She thought that maybe someday she would want a family of her own and a husband, but she had realized something about herself that summer. One reason she hadn't pushed harder for a physical relationship with Zack was that it meant leaving him would be that much more difficult. She didn't want to fall into that trap, unsure when she started thinking of it that way but she did. Maybe it was because of something Leora had said. Leora had wanted to finish her dissertation at the University of San Francisco, but didn't because she had met her grandfather and he had wanted to travel the world. How, Leora had said, could she turn that offer down? Then Camilla came along and her grandfather died shortly after. Leora made her life in Hawaii, raised her daughter alone, and became something of a philanthropist.

Leora warned Cassie not to fall in love too soon, but to live a little first. Leora wrote, "Live the life you want and make the most of it before settling down with anyone, even the love of your life, because you don't know what is going to happen. You don't know that he might die when your firstborn is just a toddler and then what do you do? Not all the money in the world will bring him back and you don't want anyone else, so you put your nose to the grindstone. You raise your daughter, you teach her and you do what your grandmother did, help the people around you when you can."

Leora's warning rang in Cassie's head all through high school, not surprising because she read and reread her grandmother's letters. Cassie told herself to be careful and not to let emotions rule her life. She especially feared that passion would overtake her, and that she would lose control of her future freedom, something she didn't intend to throw away.

She rounded the house, walked on the garden perimeter and sat on the porch swing and thought, *yes, that's what I want. I want to be able to control my own life for the first time.* Her conscience suddenly nudged her; *how honest am I being? My father said I could go to school anywhere in the world and I chose the University of Chicago.* She thought about why she made that decision and admitted at least in part the distance from Hawaii would discourage visitors. On the other hand, during her research she concluded that it must be the most exciting city in the world. She had considered New York City, but for some reason a city on a big lake, one of the Great Lakes, held more appeal to her.

Her tour of the house and gardens now complete, Cassie went to her room to get dressed for the trip and ensure her bags were ready. In 1958, people dressed smartly to travel by airplane and Cassie had a brand new traveling suit and a pillbox hat. She wasn't sure she needed the hat but all of the pictures of airline passengers showed them wearing hats, so she decided that she should have one.

She went downstairs to wait for Zack and thought about whether she should make one last attempt to his thoughts today. Their discussion a few weeks ago had been on her mind and she had pretty much dismissed the entire question about liking boys rather than girls. She rationalized it this way; if he had liked boys rather than girls, wouldn't he have shown some indication of that in high school? She didn't know how to make sense of it as this represented new territory to her. She waited on the porch until finally he pulled up in front of the house. She ran in to say goodbye to Mr. Takamura as Zack loaded her bags into the car. She would miss Mr. T., as he had always done things for her that no one else had, like make her special cakes and leave her little notes. Even in high school, he would often pack her lunch because he knew she shouldn't eat from the street vendors like many of the other kids did. She had her own plate lunch, made just for her and that always made her feel special.

She ran back out to the car, more emotional than she thought she would be, jumped in next to Zack and commanded, "Airport, driver, let's go."

But Zack said, "Now Cassie, I plan on coming into the airport and waiting with you. There's lots of time, and we can have lunch. Is that okay with you?"

"Sure, I would love that." She gave his arm a little squeeze. "You know I am more nervous about this than I thought. I mean I know my great aunt is meeting me at the airport and I will stay with her until the dormitories open up, but I never met her and I have no idea what she's like."

Zack laughed, "Hey, if she's anything like Leora, you know you are going to be in good hands." Yes, she thought that was true, although her great aunt was a good fifteen years younger than Leora. But they had the same parents and surely she there would be some similarities. Cassie explained, "All I know is that she is a widow and has a lot of money and that she had invited me to stay with her, but my father explained that I wanted to live on campus."

They traveled the rest of the 30-minute drive to the Honolulu airport in silence. She took his hand as he parked the car in the lot. "Zack, I need to tell you something that has been on my mind." He turned to look at her, as serious as ever. "I know we talked about us and our special bond, but the other day I thought that maybe we should have tried to have a physical relationship so that we would know, once and for all, if we were meant for each other or if we should just always be friends."

He smiled at her, "You mean like an experiment? Seriously, Cass, I don't think that's how it works. Hey, you aren't the only one who has been thinking, you know. I want you to know that if you meet someone, anyone who you feel that way about, I want you to explore it. Maybe that's a different kind of experiment, but I don't want you to hold back on your life because of me. You know that has always been our agreement." She nodded. Since they were kids they had an agreement that if one of them fell in love with someone

143

it would be okay with the other, no questions asked. Why, she wondered, did everything have to be so complicated now?

"Zack, will you at least kiss me goodbye so I have something to remember?" Before she finished saying it he took her in his arms, kissed her sweetly and gently on the mouth, and then slowly held her out, away from him.

"You are one smart cookie Cassie," he said, "But I think we both have to go to school, just like we planned and see if our bond will hold over the next four years."

Cassie made a face, "Ugh, Zack, that sounds so mature of you. I'm not sure if I am that mature."

He shrugged and said, "Or have you considered that maybe we are both just weird?" Relieved, she laughed and they made their way into the airport. She thought she would write him every day and tell him everything, as she always had, and without reading his thoughts, she knew he thought he would write her every day too.

As it turned out, neither one of them did.

21

Chicago

A s soon as Cassie walked down the terminal ramp, she knew which woman was her Great-Aunt Clare. Tall like Leora, with snow-white hair pulled into a tight French twist, she stood slightly apart from the crowd. Cassie thought she must have been a very striking woman in her day because her smooth skin and bright eyes still stood out. She waved to signal her and her great aunt nodded and then walked regally toward her. They didn't exactly embrace, but Aunt Clare smiled sweetly, patted her arm and welcomed her to Chicago. Cassie couldn't help but compare it to her first meeting with Leora, and she smiled at the thought of Aunt Clare jumping out of Lulubell just as Leora had that day.

"Cassandra, do you mind if I continue to call you by your given name?" she inquired as they made their way with the chauffer to the luggage area.

"Of course I wouldn't mind," Cassie replied.

"Good. As I had no news of you since Leora passed away, I have always thought of you as Cassandra, although I understand your nickname is Cassie. I just couldn't believe my eyes when I read your father's letter, and learned that you were coming to Chicago."

Not a surprise actually, Cassie thought when you have a family that never talks about anything. She almost fainted when her father told her that she had a great aunt alive who lived in Chicago.

"Come along now, we have a lot of catching up to do."

"I am so honored to be staying with you Aunt Clare, and I am anxious to know more about you and about growing up with Grandmother Leora."

Clare laughed. Cassie could hear a bit of Leora in it, and it made her smile. "Oh, I dare say those are quite interesting stories." They settled into the large limousine.

Cassie thought, *maybe I could get used to this.* The next week became a blur as her great aunt took her to see the Chicago sights. They began with a campus tour, which Cassie found overwhelming, sightseeing at the Navy Pier, the Museum of Science and Industry and finally shopping on State Street. Cassie had never been shopping in so many stores, many of which she had only seen advertised in magazines. She had a new bank account and her father had taught her how to write checks, watch her expenditures and calculate her balance. It made her feel very much like an adult and in control of her life.

Clare had convinced her that she needed a different wardrobe for Chicago, and after all, she had no argument as she knew the weather in the Midwest differed greatly from the islands. Aunt Clare loved to shop and knew what girls on campus would be wearing and the two of them had fun shopping at Marshall Field's. Cassie came away with a new fall coat, beautiful tweed jackets and new shoes.

When it came time to move into the dorms, Cassie began to feel like a fish out of water. Of course, she had made some girlfriends in Honolulu, but for most of her life she only had one close friend in Zack. She had a nagging feeling that she had been as isolated in Honolulu as she had been all those years on that Maui hilltop. She knew that most girls were concerned with hairstyles, clothes and boys, but unfortunately, those weren't her interests. Truthfully, high school had been kinder to her than grade school. She got along with most of the girls in her classes, and although there were a couple of girls that she could call friends she had never confided in them. She knew they never confided in her. Once again, she thought if she made one friend that might be enough.

All of these thoughts were swimming in her mind on the day she moved into her dormitory hall. Chase Hall, an old building hand made of solid limestone, didn't show as well on the inside where the hallways and rooms were old and sparse. The central meeting spaces were comfortably furnished and Cassie could tell well used by the girls. The first evening in the dorm a small group of girls asked if she would like to join them as they were going to the student union for something to eat. She automatically said yes, because she remembered Leora's advice, to say yes if anyone invited you. She knew from experience that after a while they wouldn't bother to ask.

Her objective in looking the part of a modern college coed was to fit in, to belong. Part of her knew that spending so much time alone with Zack had only confirmed that no one else understood her, instead of teaching her how to meet new people and make friends. Yes, she knew that to be part of the problem and yet she didn't know how to correct it.

Her roommate finally arrived, a girl who hailed from the Midwest and found everything about college exciting. Mary Ann immediately wanted to know which schools Cassie had applied for and why she had chosen Chicago and what sororities she planned to pledge, what classes she had chosen and soon Cassie had a headache. Mary Ann laughed, "I know, I know, I talk too much, but I want to hear about you. Tell me about growing up in Hawaii; do they have cars and stores there? I mean how primitive is it? Do you wear regular clothes or grass skirts or what?"

Cassie winced at the questions. So others thought of Hawaii as primitive. She thought Mary Ann meant well, at least she expressed interest. She decided that a good goal for her would be to educate Mary Ann, and as it turned out, most of her classmates were just as ignorant of post-WWII Hawaii. She had made up her mind that she would learn how to be friends with girls and not pay any attention to boys, no matter what. First, because she realized she had no real experience dating, and Zack didn't count. She also meant what she had said to him. She didn't want anything to come between them while away at college. If they decided to go their separate ways that was one thing, but she didn't want to go looking for trouble. Anyway, she didn't need a boyfriend or even a male friend, for that matter.

This seemed like a wonderful plan and later Cassie could understand why in her naivete it seemed so. She hadn't met anyone yet. Summer hadn't yet turned into fall, so the first few weeks everyone sat on the campus lawns in-between classes. After her English class, Cassie took her books and found a spot to wait for her next class. Surprisingly she enjoyed her classes and seemed to get along well with Mary Ann, although who wouldn't, she thought, as she smiled at her roommate's outgoing personality.

Although she had been in Chicago for over two months, she had written Zack only one letter. She had rationalized that he had only sent her one, so he couldn't be angry with her for not writing more often. She did miss him and she thought about him quite a lot, especially when she wanted to tell him something and couldn't. She practiced daily journaling and she thought that maybe she should use that time to write to him. She realized that half the time she wrote in her journal it was as if she were speaking to Zack.

Cassie sighed and looked over the campus grounds. Students appeared to congregate in convenient groups, the girls were all dressed in the same version of clothing, only in different colors or patterns. Most of them wore their hair in similar fashion; bobs, not curly hair chunked on top of their heads like hers.

A masculine voice interrupted her thoughts. "Do you mind if I sit here?" She looked up to see a very athletic man with blond hair and a varsity sweater over his blue button-down oxford. She stammered a bit and finally got out, "Of course, go ahead, please do." She thought to herself, *good grief, Cass.*

Smiling a movie-star smile at her, he stuck his hand out as he sat down, "I am Theo Braxton, and you are?" She took his hand and stammered, "I am Cassandra Bartholomew, but everyone calls me Cassie."

"Wow, Cassandra Bartholomew, that's quite an impressive name. You a freshman?"

"Yes, goodness, can you tell?" She couldn't help staring at him. She had never seen anyone with hair that color, like straw with a bit of honey pulled through on top. She thought he had brown eyes, but then she noticed they were green with flecks of gold in them. She had difficulty finding her voice.

"Where are you from?" he casually asked as he got out a notebook and textbook.

"I'm from Hawaii." She expected the reaction she now had become accustomed to receiving; most people were impressed because it seemed exotic and far away, but few people had ever been there. Stupid questions generally followed their initial reaction.

"Which island?" he asked. A new surprise question, most of the people she had met didn't know enough to ask which island.

"Actually two. I grew up on Maui and just moved from Oahu."

"Cool," Theo said, now writing in his notebook, as if that response contained more than enough information. Cassie saw a girl with extremely shiny, coal-black hair walking toward them.

Ignoring Cassie, she glared down at Theo. "Theo, where have you been? I thought you said we should meet over by Old Main and that's where I have been waiting for the past half hour."

Without looking up, Theo said, "Oh, sorry. Hey Janice, I want you to meet Cassie, she's a freshman and I invaded her grass space to make a note before class. Sit down here for a minute and wait for me." Reluctantly Janice sat, but she didn't look happy to be sitting with the freshman girl with un-bobbed hair.

Janice looked at her as if she were studying her closely. "What hall are you in Cassie?"

"I'm in one of the freshman dorms, Chase Hall."

"Oh." Janice said as if it took all of her energy to ask that one question. She looked away and waved at some other girls down the way. "Hey Theo, there's Carol and Barbara. I'm going to catch up with them. See you after class."

"Goodbye, Janice." He said brusquely, as he continued writing in his notebook. As soon as she left, he looked at Cassie. "Sorry, you know how sorority girls are. Anyway, I'm done and I have to get to class." She again found herself staring at him and thought *I don't have anything to say to him except he is the most handsome man I have ever seen.* Finally she stood up and said "Oh, yes, me too."

"Well, Miss Cassandra Bartholomew, nice to meet you and share your grassy spot. If you have time come over the union tonight and I'll buy you a beer."

Embarrassed for some reason she said, "Thanks Theo, I, well I can't yet, you know I'm actually only 18."

He laughed and started walking backwards, "Oh, that's right, I forgot. Well, see you around; maybe we can catch a movie together some time." He turned to walk away. She nodded and waved as he walked away, but he didn't get very far before a couple of other boys came up and walked with him. Cassie found herself looking after him, fascinated and thinking he had to be a junior at least.

Once the initial spell wore off, she gave herself a good old-fashioned Leora style talking to, starting with, "What is the matter with you? Why did you just sit there stick still and not say anything? He must think you are a total idiot." The scolding didn't make her feel any better about herself, as she walked along in a dream-like state. She couldn't get those green-gold eyes or his smile out of her mind. She had never felt this kind of excitement before and she wanted it to continue. How could she have lived this long and never felt anything like this? Had she lived at all? Cassie continued to walk as if in a daze and finally arrived at the library. She thought of the library as her hiding place; as someone who had lived quietly with a great deal of time to herself, she found it comforting compared to her dormitory and certainly compared to her room.

She decided that today she would write Zack. She had been thinking about it and she had always made excuses for why she didn't have time to write. Taking a lesson from her grandmother, she decided that every day after she wrote in her journal, her way of grounding herself for the upcoming day, she would pen a note to him. She considered telling Zack how she felt when Theo talked to her, but she distracted herself by thinking about Leora's writing system. Years ago when she first received Leora's letters she noticed that over the course of time she would make little notes of things to tell Cassie, and then she would make those notes into her letters. She knew this because Leora hadn't bothered to rewrite them; she simply wrote the letter below her scribbles. Even now, Cassie could see Leora in the little shack writing notes, but she saw her as a much younger version of the woman she had known. Even though she could see that scene with the birds and all of the familiar smells, she could never envision her mother there as a child. Once again, her daydreaming prevented her from writing to Zack, so she shook it off and began. Aware that her encounter with Theo might have something to do with her sudden desire to write to Zack, perhaps she feared change after all. She had been adamant on coming to Chicago and making a new life for herself all on her own. She wondered if the desire to have a life of her own was her heart's true desire or just a juvenile whim.

The fall continued into the season it promised to be, with colors and leaves and the brisk air off the lake. Cassie thought about joining a sorority like her roommate, and then decided against it. She justified it by saying she planned to spend a lot of time studying, so she didn't want to commit to social events. She did make it a point to attend the major campus events, and the parties afterward. In order to fit in, she made an effort to make friends with a couple of girls like herself in the dorm – girls who were more interested in their studies than a social life.

She thought about the warm air at home, always pleasant on her skin, but decided that she definitely liked the cooler air off the lake. One night after studying at the library, she noticed that her light jacket even with a sweater wouldn't keep her warm for much longer. She thought it would rain, but as she looked up, she saw the lightest dusting of snow. For someone used to snow, this early dusting in mid-November was no big deal; it melted as soon as it hit the warm ground. To Cassie, it was something magical. She walked the long way back to her dorm because she didn't want it to end. As she came in the room, Mary Ann sat at her desk studying, her long black hair up in a ponytail. Cassie burst into the room, excited. "Mary Ann, Mary Ann, look! It's snowing outside. Come, look, look right now. Isn't it fantastic?" She opened the curtain to show her.

"Are you kidding me Cassie? I grew up in northern Wisconsin. Believe me, this won't seem so wonderful about February when we have piles of it." Mary Ann resumed her studying, not even bothering to look up.

"Mary Ann, listen to me. Imagine you had never seen snow before. Wouldn't you find it amazing? I couldn't have imagined it would be this beautiful…" Cassie broke off, mesmerized by the snowflakes as they sparkled in the streetlight.

"Humph" said Mary Ann, "Trust me, I am just telling you it gets old fast."

22

M ost of the students were going home for Thanksgiving. Cassie had planned on staying at her Aunt's apartment, but about two weeks before the break her new friend, Mitzi, a girl from a city on the "north shore" invited her for the weekend. Cassie had met Mitzi the first week of school when they were both moving into the same floor in the dorm, and their friendship had blossomed because they spent so much time in the library together. Mitzi planned to earn a Master's in Library Science because she said she couldn't live without books. She was a shorter girl, rather thin with dark blonde hair, or dishwater blonde, as Cassie had heard others refer to it. Her nose had a sprinkle of light-colored freckles and she wore cute round glasses that made Cassie want to wear them. At first, she said no to Mitzi, but her persistence paid off and finally Cassie agreed.

Mitzi had four older brothers and a younger sister, and they lived in Glen Ellyn, Illinois, where her father practiced medicine. As they walked into the house from the ride they got from a friend of Mitzi's, her mother came out from the kitchen to greet them. Cassie immediately concluded that she must be the hit of the country club. Trim and fit, she looked like a model in a beige double cashmere sweater set and tailored slacks. Mitzi introduced her, "Mom, this is Cassandra Bartholomew. Cassie, this is my Mom. Her name is Deanna but you can call her Mom, all our friends do."

Cassie suddenly felt a little awkward when she realized she had never stayed with a friend before.

"I am glad to meet you Mrs. Martin." She held out her hand, but before she could stop her, Mrs. Martin reached out and gave her a big hug. Cassie thought it a very hearty hug for someone so slender.

"Cassie, you make this your home for the weekend. We always have a big meal tomorrow for Thanksgiving. Then everyone spends the afternoon watching and playing football, but you just do whatever makes you feel comfortable, all right?"

Cassie smiled and nodded, thinking how comfortable she felt already. "I, I hope I can help you with getting ready for tomorrow Mrs. Martin, although I don't have much experience. We never celebrated Thanksgiving at home so I am not familiar with the holiday, but I would like to learn."

"Really?" Mitzi said as she helped herself to some cookies on the counter. "You never celebrated Thanksgiving? That is just weird." Cassie felt she should explain as they sat down to the light supper Deanna had waiting for them. The house, a sprawling California style brick ranch, reminded Cassie of ones had seen in the movies. Mrs. Martin served them some wonderful smelling chicken vegetable soup in cups along with ham sandwiches.

"Mitzi, let me explain. There's only my father and me at home. On Thanksgiving Day, my father's habit is to go to his office in the morning and then in the evening we would have a light dinner. To me it didn't feel any different from any other day except our cook usually had the holiday off. "Wow, you had a cook?" Mitzi exclaimed, "How cool!" Cassie felt that maybe she should keep any future explanations of her upbringing to herself. Just then, one very muscular young man and then another came into the kitchen talking loudly about some football player. Cassie stopped in mid-sentence with what she had started to say and stared at them.

Mrs. Martin laughed when she saw Cassie's reaction. "Cassie, these very rude young men are my two of my sons, both home from school and both always in the kitchen underfoot."

They both turned to look at Cassie with smiles and nods. "This is Joe and John and tomorrow you will meet the twins; Matthew and Michael," Mitzi added as she jumped up to elbow Joe and poke John. "It's always a mad house here during the holidays, because we all drop in on Mom and Dad and act just like we did when we were kids."

Her mother added, "What she means, Cassie, is that we are a very loud and noisy family and everyone teases and talks over everyone else." Mrs. Martin's description proved to be accurate. Later that evening when she met the twins Cassie could see that although the twin brothers had darker hair, they were younger versions of the older two. They were not identical twins so that proved a relief to Cassie, who was having trouble keeping everyone straight.

She liked Mitzi's Dad, a tall, distinguished man with silver hair and a welcoming and friendly manner; Cassie could immediately see why he made a great doctor. That evening she asked Mitzi, "What kind of a doctor is your Dad?"

Mitzi replied, "He is a cardiologist, you know a heart doctor. What he mostly does is operate on people with heart problems. Hmm, that's a weird question I guess no one ever asked me that before." Cassie made a note to herself that if her symptoms had truly returned she should see a doctor to determine if she required treatment again. Certainly not the Maui hilltop treatment, but treatment nonetheless.

On Thanksgiving Day Cassie and Mitzi helped Deanna in the large country kitchen. The brothers set up the tables, not only in the dining room but also in the living room including a smaller card table as the "kid's table." Mitzi's younger sister had spent the morning complaining loudly that she shouldn't have to sit with all of her little cousins because she was nine. Her mother, exasperated, finally said, "Janie, I told you before. I need you at that table. Your job is to supervise your three cousins; you know how crazy they can get at dinner." Pacified for the moment, Janie went off to make place cards. When dinner finally came, Cassie could barely take it all in, with the noise of everyone teasing, joking, and talking over everyone else. This scene presented a new concept for Cassie, who began to understand she had been not only on an island; she had been isolated from family life as well.

The other thing entirely new to her was church. Although Mr. Mister had come to see her every week when she lived on Maui, most of the time they didn't talk about God or what it meant to believe in him.

They simply talked about Bible stories or whatever else Cassie had on her mind. When she returned to live with her father, he never brought it up and neither did she. In fact, she never even thought about church or God. On Thanksgiving morning, as she sat in the Martin's church she watched carefully and followed as they sat or stood and bowed their heads in prayer. Later Dr. Martin said a long prayer before dinner about how wonderful God's blessings were and how thankful everyone should be for good health, family, and friends.

Then, to Cassie's amazement, they went around the table and each person identified the number one thing for which they were grateful. Sitting there, Cassie began to panic, with no idea what she could contribute. When her turn came, she took a deep breath, looked into her lap and slowly said, "I am grateful that I am able to experience Thanksgiving with such a wonderful family." Everyone clapped and she felt herself becoming red in the face, but with pleasure, not embarrassment.

That afternoon, after they had cleaned everything up, the boys watched football. Then Joe told everyone to get ready for the annual football game. In the midst of a flurry of activity, Mitzi shouted to Cassie to get her coat and come outside with her. Sidling up to her, Cassie said quietly, "Please Mitzi, I have no idea how to do anything like this, and I'll look stupid." Mitzi frowned at her, "What do you mean, you don't know how to throw a ball? Don't be silly, Cassie, it's a lot of fun."

Cassie lied, "Well, of course I know how to throw and catch a ball, I have just never played football." Mitzi smiled, "Is that what you are worried about? It's only flag football, don't worry, we don't usually tackle anyone." She grabbed Cassie's coat, threw it to her and pulled her out the door.

Out in the yard as Cassie watched Mitzi interact with her brothers and a few neighborhood friends, once again she had a picture of how much she had missed in her life. Lost in her thoughts, she didn't see Michael, one of the twins, come up behind her and pick her up off the ground. She screamed and he put her down quickly. She turned to look at him. "Come on Cassie, you have got to get into this game." He took her hand and pulled her into the group, smiling and winking at her. Cassie laughed and joined in after all, Michael's wink not lost on her. Later that night after Mr. and Mrs. Martin had retired, everyone sat in the comfortable family room in front of the fire. Mitzi sat closest to the fire, making S'mores and Michael immediately sat on the big couch right next to Cassie. In this loud talkative group, no one paid much attention to them. Michael wanted to know about her life in Hawaii, how she found the University and the differences she noticed. He was very skilled at getting her to share and Cassie soon felt so comfortable that she leaned into him as she described her life on Maui and then on Oahu. Eventually everyone left for bed and Cassie noticed that although the fire had almost gone out the two of them were still talking.

"Guess we should go to bed too, Michael." She yawned and stood up.

"Why Cassie, you are very forward for a freshman."

Cassie stopped, unsure of the joke at first and then she laughed, "Don't be silly Michael Martin, you know what I meant." He came toward her and when he stood in front of her, she became aware of how he towered above her. He gently took her hands in his. "Would you be willing to go out with me some time when we are back at school?" Awkward and embarrassed, instead of answering him she pulled away, took her sweater and started upstairs. Realizing her mistake, she called back to him in a loud whisper, "Oh, of course I will."

That night, lying in bed in Mitzi's room, Cassie decided she sincerely meant what she had said at the dinner table, that she felt gratitude for the opportunity to be with this family. By contrast she saw her life with her father as quite a lonely existence, and wondered what her life would have been if her mother had lived or at least if she had a brother or sister. While thinking those thoughts, she fell sound asleep.

Dreams of church, God, and Michael Martin – although he looked more like Zack in her dream – woke her in the early dawn light. She thought, *what could any of that mean?* However, she rolled over and went back to sleep. They were going shopping tomorrow and Cassie already felt drained.

23

O n Sunday morning, the family again readied themselves to go to church and Cassie didn't feel well. Yesterday when they were shopping, she had that familiar feeling again, as if she were going to faint. She knew that her heart should be well, as her doctor had declared when she was in grade school, but she had infrequent bouts with fainting through high school whenever she over-exerted herself. She had never told her father because she believed she knew how to manage it, but over the last month, the episodes had become more frequent and now they frightened her.

As she came into the kitchen to join the Martins for breakfast, the entire family seemed to turn and look at her. Mrs. Martin asked, "Cassie dear, are you feeling well? You look very tired."

Cassie steadied herself on the chair. "I'm sorry Mrs. Martin, I guess I just did too much yesterday I am not sure…" and with that, she fainted.

When Cassie opened her eyes, she looked up at Dr. Martin and Mitzi. Judging from the paneling and the certificates on the wall, she guessed this to be his home office. When she looked at Dr. Martin she felt guilty, as if she had been keeping a secret from him. She tried to read his thoughts, to revisit the old system to see if it still worked, but all she could hear were technical terms and medical questions she couldn't comprehend. "Cassie, are you able to sit up?" he asked. What a kind man, she thought and aloud she said, "Yes, of course, I'm fine."

"Cassie, please tell me the truth. Has this happened to you before?" He paused and then added, "Mitzi, would you mind getting a glass of water for her? Take your time; I would like a minute alone with Cassie."

Cassie felt herself getting warm and tears sprang to eyes. She was angry with herself for showing emotion. She looked at Dr. Martin and sighed. "It's a long story, Dr. Martin." She proceeded to tell him her story, of her time in Maui, her doctors on Oahu, what they had said and how the episodes that she thought were behind her had now returned.

Dr. Martin looked at her intently and now she heard his thoughts clearly, that because she had appeared pale and withdrawn he had first assumed a pregnancy. He wouldn't have been surprised since many college girls were sexually active. Cassie's eyes opened wide, incensed at what she had heard, but since Doctor Martin couldn't know she could read his mind she had to keep her emotions in check.

"Dr. Martin, I can assure you you do not need to concern yourself with me. I'm fine." She stood up and prepared to leave the room.

"Young lady, you need to sit right there, we are not done talking yet." Mitzi knocked on the door with the water, and Dr. Martin took the glass from her and handed it to Cassie. "Mitzi, you go on, I'll send Cassie out as soon as we're done." He sat down next to her on the couch. "Do you mean to tell me you aren't under a doctor's care now and these episodes have recently reappeared?"

"Yes," Cassie said, her eyes lowered. "I know I should have done something about it, but the last doctor I saw before I came to the mainland said he heard a little trouble, but overall I should be fine and not to worry."

Martin took her hand. "Cassie, you know that how we treat heart defects today has dramatically changed since you were a child. I think we should send for your medical records and do a complete workup here so we can pinpoint the issue and address it. That way you won't have to worry about fainting, which believe it or not, in the wrong place could be quite dangerous."

"I understand Dr. Martin, I do." She smiled and thought that although the silver in his hair made him appear to be older than her own father, he acted younger.

"Here," he said as he pulled out some papers from a desk drawer, "Let's fill this out and I'll have Mitzi let you know when I have them so we can schedule the workup. Would you like me to call your father and explain the situation to him? I would be more than glad to."

"No." She said, now terribly alarmed. "I mean, of course I will tell him myself, Dr. Martin, not a problem, thank you anyway." Her concern that she would lose complete control of the situation and her father would make her come home seemed reason enough to panic.

"All right, I will trust that you'll do that, Cassie. I want you to know I won't tell anyone about this, because no one needs to know your business. If you wish to tell Mitzi that's entirely up to you. Come along now, I think Mitzi and the others are ready to leave to return to school. I'm happy we had this talk and found out while you were here, rather than having something happen to you back at school." Happy or not, she wanted to get this issue resolved and get on with her life.

A few weeks later Mitzi came to her room with a puzzled look on her face. "Hey, Cassie, I got a note from Dad that you need to call his office. What's going on?" Cassie looked at her friend and decided to make light of it. "Remember when I fainted at your house? Your dad and I talked and he decided I should get some tests, just to be sure everything is okay and he sent for my medical records. That's all, no big deal." She picked up her books to head out to the library and Mitzi seemed to accept her explanation without further question. She breathed a sigh of relief. She hated the thought of anyone making a big deal of her fainting and even more, of her heart problems. Since Thanksgiving, she had made it a practice to get more sleep every night, difficult with winter finals approaching, but she hadn't felt like fainting again, either.

Due to work demands, her father had written that he had to change his plans and wouldn't be spending Christmas with her in Chicago after all. Since she would be spending the break at Aunt Clare's, Cassie decided she needed to tell her about the upcoming doctor appointments, but not until Christmas. It worked well because Dr. Martin had set up the appointments during the break. Cassie felt very grown up about all of this and felt relieved about making her own decisions now.

The Chicago cold weather remained a novelty to her and she hadn't tired of snow yet, as Mary Ann had predicted. She became adept at riding the El and managed to get around the city without having to depend on anyone; she cherished the feeling of independence.

She continued to write to Zack every day in her journal although she had yet to send him a letter, and there were moments when she wondered why he hadn't written, either. She didn't spend too much time thinking about it because of finals and end of semester activities. Cassie actually looked forward to spending Christmas in Chicago because it would be like Christmases she had read about, with snow and cold. One little thought kept nagging at her, that she hadn't called her father as she had promised Dr. Martin. She knew the Doctor's office would have to inform him about the record request, but she couldn't bring herself to call him. She figured as soon as she told Aunt Clare the truth she would make her call him.

The next day, sitting in the formal living room of Aunt Clare's apartment overlooking Lake Michigan, she felt very much at home. Without any reservations, she told her great aunt, now her only remnant of her mother and grandmother, everything. She told her about the fainting episodes, about not feeling well, and that Dr. Martin had arranged for the tests over the holiday break.

When she finished what had been one long run-on sentence, Aunt Clare looked at her and sighed. "I can see that this has been a burden for you to carry Cassandra. You mentioned that you haven't called your father; please explain to me your reasoning for not doing so."

"Aunt Clare, I was afraid, very afraid that he would make me come back home and see my own doctor and I didn't want to leave school right now."

Clare frowned. "Don't you think he would understand that? He should be treated with respect."

"I know Aunt Clare, that's why I wanted to talk to you first. You see my father and I don't… we don't communicate very well and I thought if you were in my corner that he wouldn't insist on my coming home right now."

"Of course I am in your corner, what a thing to say. Let's call him together. I can be here with you and I'm sure that all will be well; however, I have one condition for doing this. I will come with you to these appointments. I won't have you hiding anything else from me."

As it turned out, Cassie shouldn't have been so concerned. Her father sounded quite content to allow Aunt Clare to accompany her to the doctor and in fact, Cassie thought she sensed relief in his voice. She couldn't read his mind over the phone and she told herself she shouldn't speculate about what the reason could be, but it made her suspect he was hiding something. She told him that the appointments would be in early January and agreed to call him as soon as they had results.

24

C assie had the best time in the tinsel and light-filled world of downtown Chicago at Christmas. She never tired of looking at the window displays. Clearly, Marshall Fields' were the most impressive. Aunt Clare loved to shop and have lunch at the Walnut Room there. The two of them became almost as close as Cassie and Leora had been. In addition, she had finally heard from Zack. Quite a long letter arrived that provided detail about his classes at University of Hawaii at Manoa, their friends, the beach and all the news from back home. Toward the end, he slipped in the fact that he hadn't done much socially, but planned to try out for the swim team. He sounded excited about that possibility.

Zack's letter finally nudged Cassie into taking her daily journal notes and composing a letter to him. It took her the better part of an afternoon and once she began writing she found she couldn't stop. She left out a few things, of course; no need to worry him about her fainting episodes or the upcoming medical appointments. She also didn't mention the boys she had met or the couple of dates she had with Michael Martin after the Thanksgiving break. They were harmless dates, with no kissing or anything, so she thought it best not to mention it. She wondered if he had actually dated anyone and if he too conveniently left that part out of his letter.

Since pen and paper were in front of her, she thought she should be a good daughter and write her father a letter. Frankly, it had never occurred to her that he would want one, but when she and Aunt Clare called him, he had commented about how nice it would be if she wrote him about campus details, her classes and so on. It felt like a mild admonition, and she thought she should comply. She knew that he expected her to do well so she didn't even mention grades, but she did explain in detail her curricula because she knew of his interest. She went on in some detail about the various museums, describing the Art museum and the Shedd Aquarium in detail. Finally, she thought she would make a little story for him about how many people she met had the strangest notions about life in Hawaii. She couldn't believe many of the odd notions existed; since the end of the war many pictures, newsreels, and other information about the islands were available. Maybe in time that would change people's ignorance, she explained.

As she sat there, pen in hand, she thought of her father as a puzzle, a mystery to her and that it had always been that way. Willing to answer questions to a point, but then very clearly, as if she could almost see it, the door would shut and she would be on the outside. When her father visited her in Maui, she didn't know any different and accepted him as he was, and when she lived with him in Honolulu, she accepted that their relationship consisted of pleasantries of the day. When she met Leora she began to understand how life and relationships could be with people you love. On the day they spread Leora's ashes she experienced the only tender moment she ever shared with her Father; after that it was as if he had never opened the door to her at all. She came to accept that love or not, her relationship with her Father would never change. Lately there were moments when she wondered what it would be like to have someone like Dr. Martin for a father or Mrs. Martin for a mother. She didn't allow herself those thoughts for long because then she would wonder if she had ever experienced real love at all. Nothing could have prepared her for the surprise her father had in store for her.

Aunt Clare got the call and as she hung up the phone, she turned to look at Cassandra, speechless. Finally, she said slowly and deliberately, "Cassandra, your father is coming to Chicago, and he's not coming alone. Evidently, he has met someone and he is going to be married. He is coming here so that you can meet her." Even stoic Aunt Clare looked shocked at the news.

Cassie's mouth dropped open and she began to laugh because she thought it the strangest news she had ever heard. "Oh, Aunt Clare, how he has surprised us! Now we are going to have some fun, aren't we?" She truly meant it. Life certainly had taken some unusual turns lately and she had begun to appreciate the unknowns of the road that lay ahead of her.

True to her word Aunt Clare did not allow Cassie go to any medical appointments without her. It turned out to be a good thing because by the time they finished with all of the recommended tests and procedures Cassie was glad she had insisted. At last, she and Aunt Clare waited in Dr. Martin's downtown office, both nervous with anticipation about her test results. Dr. Martin himself came to get them, gracious as ever as he introduced himself to Aunt Clare and showed them into a conference room. Cassie tried to calm herself with the thought that no matter what the results were, she would stay in school. Dr. Martin took her shaking hands in his, looked her straight in the eyes and said, "Cassie, I want you to relax because all of this is good news, my girl. Now breathe for me." Cassie let out her breath, unaware that she had been holding it. They all laughed and Dr. Martin smiled at her and said, "You know Cassie, holding your breath can make you faint. Now, please listen carefully to me. First, the good news. Your heart defect, which is what originally had doctors concerned, has completely healed and there is absolutely no reason for you to be concerned anymore." Cassie stared at him unable to comprehend what he had said.

"But, Dr. Martin, the fainting, why has it returned?"

"You know Cassie, when you were a little girl they didn't have the same tests we have today; fortunately your fainting has nothing to do with your heart." Now even more confused, Cassie felt the tears well up. "Let me continue." Dr. Martin added, "Remember, this is all good news. Cassie, you happen to have abnormally low blood pressure, which can result in fainting on occasion. I am sorry to tell you that there's probably no treatment available, but you do need to be aware of your blood pressure. It may be a good idea to learn what triggers it. For example, when you were at the house for Thanksgiving, it happened to be the first thing in the morning and because you were tired you got out of bed right before you came downstairs is that right? She nodded. "And I assume you also hadn't had anything to eat that morning?"

"No, I mean you are correct, I didn't eat anything and then I fainted." She considered this new information carefully and said, "Come to think of it that's usually when it happens, in the morning before I eat anything."

He patted her hand, "That's a good sign that you are already more aware. I'm going to make a full report and send it to your father with a copy for your doctor back home, although I understand Dr. Fellows is now retired. I can also call your father if it would help, would you like me to do that?"

Cassie explained that her father would be in Chicago within the week and she and Aunt Clare would explain it all to him.

Dr. Martin stood up, "Cassie, I looked forward to today. Nothing like a good medical report to cheer me up and I certainly hope you two ladies are planning on celebrating. When you have the chance Cassie, you may want to let Mitzi and the rest of the family know about your results. They are all worried and have been bothering me day and night about it. I told them the only one who could share anything would be you." He winked at her and ushered them out of the office and in the hallway.

Cassie felt tears welling up in her eyes as she turned to face Aunt Clare, who spontaneously hugged her.

"He's right, Cassie my girl, let's celebrate. I know just the place on the lake I would like to take you, even in the winter it is a lovely spot."

Cassie, still in shock, tried not to think about the obvious question, which had now pushed itself to the forefront of her mind. Did they send her to Maui for more than five years of solitude unnecessarily? She pushed it out of her mind. Nothing could stop her happiness now. The worry lifted from her heart and she could feel the excitement rising up within her as the news became a reality. Everything she couldn't do her entire life – run, swim, or exercise – all were now open to her. A smile spread across her face, "Yes, let's go celebrate Aunt Clare; there's so much joy inside me right now I could burst."

After that news, the next best part of the break came when Michael Martin took her to a show called The Ice Capades. She had never seen a live performance and she felt certain she looked all of ten years old watching the skates glide, jump, and twirl on the ice. As they walked to a nearby restaurant for a late supper Michael put his arm around her trying to keep warm in the frigid January lake air. They settled into the wooden booth of the Irish Pub he had picked and ordered soup with thick slabs of bread. As they waited for the food Michael looked intensely at her. She smiled back at him, so at ease with him, although he was three years older and about to graduate. She smiled again, "What is it Michael? Why are you staring at me?"

"Because I have so much fun showing you things you have never seen before, Cassie. Most girls wouldn't have enjoyed the Ice Capades, but you loved it and it showed."

"Why wouldn't I? I never would have imagined skating like that, probably because I have never even been skating."

Michael suddenly reached across the table and took her two hands in his. "Cassie, I have to ask you a question. Ok?"

"Sure, shoot."

"You may not know that I had a girlfriend pretty much all through high school and I always assumed that we would be together forever, but when she went to college out East something changed. She decided she didn't want to be with me anymore."

Cassie said, "Why are you telling me all of this now?" She didn't mention that she already knew about his high school girlfriend from Mitzi, including how it broke his heart to the point that he didn't date anyone until now.

"Because Cassie, I never thought I would feel anything for anyone again, at least not the way I felt about her. But you know I think you are terrific, I like you a lot and ..." He sat back and withdrew his hands not knowing exactly what to say next. Cassie thought about reading his mind to help him, but she had promised herself that it would be like interference in football and it might influence the outcome. Actually, it felt more like trespassing where she didn't belong and for that reason, she had determined to stop using The Gift. Listening to Michael struggle to explain how he felt tempted her again to read his thoughts, but she reminded herself that would mean that she didn't trust him to tell her the truth about his feelings. Their conversation ended as their food came to the table.

As they walked back to the car, the snow crunching underfoot, Cassie said, "Michael stop," and he turned to her, "I need to tell you something about myself too."

Michael looked down at her and with one hand lifted her chin so that she would look at him. "I already know everything I need to know about you Cassie B." He put his mouth on hers, kissed her softly, and then put his arms around her little frame as she sunk into them happily. As he felt her relax against him he pulled away to look at her. "Alright, now my curiosity has kicked in. What did you want to tell me about you?"

"Wow, I can't remember." she paused, "Michael, you are probably not going to believe this, but I have only had one other kiss in my life. No one has ever held me like this, and now..." Her voice trailed off and she looked away from the intensity of his eyes, unused to the feelings that were coming along with the heat of his gaze.

He laughed and hugged her again, "That's exactly it Cassie girl. That's what I tried to say earlier, I like you because you are just so doggone honest." He took her in his arms again and kissed her, and this time not as politely.

25

E xcept for one excursion with her aunt, she spent every remaining day of the holiday break with Michael. Cassie had never felt this way and worried that the relationship might be getting serious, but on the other hand, she didn't care because time flew with him.

One night while still at her aunt's apartment she saw the Menehune. It had been a long time and even as she slept, she wondered what it meant. The little old man stood in front of her, winked, and motioned for her to come forward. She followed him into the dark tropical woods she now recognized as the upper Nuuanu Valley, not Maui. As she followed him, she sensed it getting darker and darker and other creatures were around them, but she didn't feel fear. They finally came to a clearing and she could see the Menehune all around her; young and old and out of the middle came the bright green light. She put out her hand and she expected to see the little dragon but instead she could see a bird, the smallest of the hummingbirds. As it buzzed in midair, it gave off a greenish blue light, and then lit on her finger and looked at her. Just as she would have asked the dragon without speaking she asked, "Are you warning me?" The hummingbird took off and buzzed around her head, and then around the Menehune, eventually settling on the top of her head. She tried to keep very still and then she heard his words. *Be careful Cassie, be careful or you'll get your heart broken. Love, but don't love too much. Give, but only if it is given in return."* She could have sworn it sounded like Leora. Cassie opened her eyes, sat up straight in bed and concluded that the visit wasn't a warning of evil or danger, merely a grandmotherly warning to be careful about falling in love too quickly. She pictured Michael and thought nothing bad would ever happen with him. And then she went back to sleep.

Spring finally arrived in the Midwest and with it a sudden late snowstorm. The strong winds off Lake Michigan made it seem to Cassie as if the dull grey winter of March would never end. As she walked around campus in her old boots, tired of the mess and the chill, she hoped that April would be better. April only brought more grey, with endless rain. The only bright spot in her life was Michael and she knew she had better think about the future or summer would be here, he would be gone and she wouldn't know what would happen to them.

One evening after Michael dropped her off at her dorm she ran up the flights of steps to her room, glad she no longer had to take them slowly. She had never experienced such intense feelings and she wanted to be alone with them. She was relieved as she opened the door and saw that Mary Ann hadn't yet returned. She left the lights off and using the bit of light that entered the room from the parkway she took off her clothes and got into bed, ensuring that even when Mary Ann came in she wouldn't have to talk to her. Her heart felt as if it could sing, singing inside of her, and singing a song that she couldn't remember where or when she learned it, but it existed in her heart:

By the light of the moon,
By the silvery sea,
Girl, I've got you,
And you've got me.

She repeated it to herself and hugged her knees to her chest. *Why didn't I ever feel this way with Zack,* she wondered. There were similarities between both men; she knew Zack cared about her, she had fun with him and they never ran out of things to talk about. Although the same could be said for her time with Michael, something indescribable in her heart felt different with him. She lay there bathed in the wonderfulness of it all, and thought how she never wanted it to end.

Even the upcoming unexpected and mysterious visit of her father couldn't shake Cassie's feelings of warmth and happiness when Michael was around. He planned to marry, but what did it matter? She had her life; her schoolwork, her wonderful aunt and now she had Michael. When she thought of Zack and that she hadn't heard from him, she told herself it didn't matter because they would always be friends, no matter what.

The meeting with her father and his fiancee took place one rainy April evening at the Drake Hotel on Chicago's famed Golden Mile. Her father hadn't seen Clare for years and she hadn't understood why until she observed them together. They met in the hotel lobby and as they anxiously waited for Hannah to join them, Cassie noticed how coldly Aunt Clare, usually such a warm woman, treated her father. She seemed almost as if she were angry, but Cassie dismissed it as her imagination and then she spotted Hannah descending the stairs. While she knew her father had met her at his law firm, when she had clerked for him, she found herself unprepared for how young and beautiful she was. In the few minutes before Hannah arrived, she had observed her father looked happy, although she had no idea what that would look like on him. He had become thinner and had shaved so closely she thought he looked at least ten years younger than the last time she had seen him.

After brief introductions, they headed into the hotel's dining room, lavishly decorated with red velvet walls and white table linens. The crystal centerpieces contained deep wine colored roses and white baby's breath, and there were tall white candles on every table. While her father ordered wine for the table, she took a good look at Hannah, who appeared to be nervous and sat as close as she could to her father. It became apparent that they were holding hands under the table. Aunt Clare started the conversation bluntly, "I assume, Hannah, that you would like to get to know a bit about our family." *Smart,* Cassie thought, *rather than making it all about her, which after all it clearly is.*

Cassie sat back in her chair, thinking that Aunt Clare, a great storyteller, would begin. Instead, she turned to her. "Cassandra, why don't you tell Hannah all about yourself, how you came to be here in Chicago and what you hope to accomplish here."

Cassie sighed, thought she might as well get it over with, and quickly covered her early life in Maui, her time back on Oahu and her brief experience in Chicago.

She stopped when she came to Michael and wondered, *what should I say about him?* Fortunately, she was saved when the wine arrived and the sommelier poured for everyone, including her.

Hannah's eyes widened, "Cassie, I had no idea you had gone through all of that. Andrew hadn't shared any of your early life with me." She turned to look at him smiled lovingly. Cassie thought, *great, I haven't even been a topic of conversation between the two of them.* Then she wondered why he had made this visit. "Hannah that's really all there is to know about me and I don't think it's all that interesting. Why don't you tell us more about you, how you came to be in Hawaii, and how you met Andrew, I mean Father."

Hannah laughed, and shook her head back so that her long blonde hair got everyone's attention.

"I'm a Minnesota girl. My entire family is from Norway and that's where I get my Scandinavian looks. After I attended St. Olaf's, I moved to California to study law. When I looked for an internship or clerking position, something about the advertisement from your father's firm intrigued me. From the first time we spoke on the phone, something clicked. As a result, I didn't entertain any other offers; I bought my plane ticket and moved to Oahu. After a few months, Andrew finally got up the nerve to ask me out for a drink. Even though it isn't a good idea to fraternize with the boss, I agreed. We had been working together closely on a case and I admired his thought process, and I learned so much from him." She said most of this looking at Andrew as if he were the only one who mattered. "Anyway," she continued, "From that day on, things moved quickly and after only dating for a month he asked me to marry him and join the firm full time."

What kind of a marriage proposal was that? Cassie thought, and she saw Aunt Clare raise one eyebrow as well. She could see that Aunt Clare prepared to make a statement. "Andrew, it is very nice to bring Hannah all the way to Chicago, but you have been a widower for what, seventeen years now? Surely you don't need anyone's permission to marry?"

Cassie thought, *well that's my Aunt Clare all right, glad that she had come right out and asked him exactly what she wanted to know.* Her father didn't look a bit sheepish or embarrassed at Aunt Clare's words, instead he looked at Hannah, smiled and turned back to the two of them.

"Clare, Cassie, perhaps no one understands what my life consisted of for the past seventeen years. It was nothing but work and worry. Yes, my constant worry about losing Cassie as I lost Camilla. She came home to Oahu at a terrible time for the practice. I thought we would have time together to get to know each other, but by then she was and remained as closed as I had been." He sighed and looked at Cassie, who looked away. She didn't want to open these doors; she didn't want to have this conversation.

Hannah, said "Andrew, maybe we should have dinner first and then finish this discussion."

"No, I came here to tell them, to let them know that I am alive again, not merely a shell of a man, which is exactly what I was for seventeen years. When I lost Camilla I couldn't breathe and my fear of losing Cassie made me take the drastic action I did, by sending her so far away from me. God knows Leora was so angry she wouldn't speak to me for years, but I had to trust the best medical advice available in 1945 and I simply couldn't afford to be with her, I had to make a living."

Clare interrupted him, "Oh for goodness sakes, Andrew, I understand all of that and I am sure Cassandra does too, but you still haven't answered my question, but why now, why come here now?"

Again, Andrew sighed and continued. "The truth is right before Camilla died she made me promise something. I never thought about that promise, actually I never told anyone about it, because I didn't think it necessary. Camilla asked me to promise not to marry again unless I had the consent of Cassie and her grandmother and since Leora is gone, well, that left you, Clare." Again, he smiled at Hannah, "I honestly never thought I would ever feel this way about someone again, and certainly not to the point of wanting to marry. As Cassie can tell you all I did the entire time she lived with me was work, taking on more and more clients with the excuse that I needed to build the firm's reputation, but truthfully it allowed me to avoid feeling. Honestly, Cassie, until I met Zack I didn't even appreciate how lonely it must have been for you, living alone with me."

Cassie, clearly exasperated said, "But what does he have to do with this?"

"Please Cassandra, be patient with me. When I saw you interact with him, I recognized something about you and our relationship. You and Zack clearly communicated, and had a strong relationship. You and I had nothing like that, and I blamed only myself."

26

The waiters arrived with their dinner and Andrew urged everyone to eat and drink some wine. "Don't worry," he said, "We are not leaving this restaurant until I have told you everything."

Cassie suddenly felt how her father's news had affected her, and she enjoyed the break to eat the wonderful meal and calm her nerves. They made small talk until they were served their last course, a Creme brulee that Cassie had never tasted before. Cassie felt compelled to speak up. "Father, I understand what you said about Mother's wishes, but what I cannot understand is why she would have made such a request of you. Why wouldn't she trust you to marry well?"

"That's as good of a place to start as any," her father said as he waited for his coffee to be served. "You probably don't know this, Cassie, but your grandmother never wanted me to marry your mother. I know Clare is aware of that." Aunt Clare nodded in affirmation. "There were at least three reasons for her objections. My family didn't enjoy the same place in society as your mother's and she had been engaged before we met. Her mother suspected that she was simply marrying on the, what do you call it?" Hannah added, "Rebound."

"Yes, on the rebound. That's one reason, and the next is a bit more complicated. Most of my life I immersed myself in my work and I didn't pay attention to women. When Camilla caught my eye, I fell desperately in love and proposed immediately, refusing a lengthy courtship. Leora made it clear that she thought we were rushing things. The third reason I suspect you already know, Cassie. Your grandmother held out hope that Camilla, unlike her, would return to the mainland and finish her studies. In the end, she couldn't stop us and we were married. When your mother fell ill, I felt it was somehow my fault. If she hadn't married me so quickly maybe she would still be alive, I know it sounds strange to say it but that's how I felt."

Clare took his hand in hers. "Dear, dear Andrew, I had no idea you blamed yourself. I only knew that Leora didn't think much of the match at the time, but I know Leora didn't blame you Andrew, you must believe that."

Tears welled up in her father's eyes, something Cassandra had only seen once before and had doubted she would see again. She felt strange sitting in the middle of this restaurant, overhearing this conversation as if she were an intruder in her father's study and finding him in a compromising position with this woman. She stood up abruptly and excused herself. At the front of the restaurant, she asked directions to the women's lounge and hurried there, worried that someone would see the tears streaming down her face. Somehow seeing all of that emotion in her father, a man she now understood she barely knew proved to be too much for her. Her heart hurt. She stood with her back against the cold white tile of the bathroom stall and let herself feel. She recalled how many times she secretly

186

hated her father, and felt anger for shutting her out. She had done the same in revenge; she had simply shut him out of her heart and certainly out of her life.

The pain caused her to sob aloud. She heard the door open, and someone come in. "Cassandra dear? Are you all right? I just thought I should check on you."

"Yes," she gulped a sob down. "I think so; I need a minute, please. I didn't mean to be rude, Aunt Clare I...." And her voice broke again with the emotion of seeing her father for the first time as a real person. "Please, I'll be there shortly. I need to compose myself and wash my face." A few minutes later, she returned to the table. As she picked up her napkin, she looked up to see the others staring at her, waiting for some kind of explanation. "I apologize to you all. I don't know what came over me. I guess this is just an emotional day for me," she said lightly and flipped her hand in the air as if she had tossed the entire episode aside.

"Please, Cassie, there's no need to apologize. This is an emotional day for us all," her father said and she wondered, as she did as a child, if her emotional outburst upset him. "I took the opportunity to pay the bill. Now, would you and Clare like to join us tomorrow to explore the city, which you seem to be enjoying."

So that's the end of the discussion. Cassie wondered if it she could ask questions or introduce any further discussion, but Aunt Clare spoke up, "Andrew I apologize, but I have bridge club tomorrow and normally I would beg off, but it is at my home so I am obligated to host."

"Of course, Clare of course. Cassie, can we count on you to be our tour guide around the city?"

Feeling more in control of herself, she quickly responded. "Of course, Father, I know it quite well and we can take taxis. I think the best plan would be for me to meet you here in the lobby, say about 9:30 a.m.?"

On that closing note they stood, and said their goodbyes with awkward kisses and hugs. Clare and Cassie went to the front to meet their driver and Andrew and Hannah went to the elevators. Once safely in her aunt's car, Cassie broke down again, sobbing uncontrollably.

Through choked sobs, she struggled to explain. "I don't think anyone understands why I am so upset, but I don't even know that man. He never, in all the years on Maui, or when I lived at home with him did he ever have one private conversation with me - ever. The only exception, the one time it happened was the day we sprinkled Leora's ashes but even after that it remained so...."

As she searched for the word Aunt Clare volunteered, "Formal? Distant? Removed?"

"Yes, yes, yes. All of the above Aunt Clare, and now when I listen to him I guess I can understand that at first he tried to protect himself from feeling any more hurt, but, Aunt Clare, he sent a five-year-old child away and right after I had lost my mother. How could he not know that it was the worst thing you could do to a child?" She continued sobbing, wiping her eyes with the soaking wet handkerchief and the back of her white gloves.

"Hush now, let's get home and we can have a long talk. This is a great deal to take in, my dear, and I doubt that you are used to feeling a lot of emotion. You need to learn to experience it a bit at a time or it will overwhelm you and you won't be able to function at all."

When they reached the apartment, Aunt Clare suggested that she get ready for bed and she would bring in some tea so they could talk. Shaking now and feeling even worse than she did in the restaurant bathroom, Cassie found she couldn't stop the tears from streaming down her face onto her neck and chest. Finally, she sat on her bed in the plaid wool pajamas her aunt had given her for Christmas. She knew that Michael expected her to call, but she felt as though she were made of lead and she sat frozen on the edge of the bed. The lights of the Chicago skyline generally soothed her, but the blackness of the lake failed to calm her.

Aunt Clare came in with a tray of tea and hot chocolate. She wore her favorite dressing gown of rose-colored chenille. "I'm embarrassed to say that I didn't know which you would prefer, so I brought both."

"Oh, Aunt Clare." Suddenly her aunt's kindness led to more crying. "You mean so much to me and I don't know what I would do without you."

"Hush now; do you want the hot chocolate or the tea? Let's talk this thing out. I must tell you your father did shock me tonight. I expected him, as I believe you did, to maintain his serious demeanor, his stoic self in spite of the cover story about his love for this girl. But his very genuine emotion and concern for you and my goodness, his sadness over his loss of any relationship with you made me actually feel well, not sorry, but I think the word is, more appreciative, of him as a person. Personally, all these years I had only thought of him as a monster."

Sensing that Cassie might start crying again, she turned to her. "Why do you think that his behavior had such an effect on you, my dear girl?" Cassie didn't answer. "Let's think about it for a minute. Are you normally much of a crier?

"Oh, no, Aunt Clare, I can't even remember when I last cried. Of course I cried a great deal when I lost Leora but other than that I didn't cry, not like this anyway."

"Then let's cut to the chase girl, before tonight how did you feel about your father?" Cassie lifted her head up to look at her Aunt Clare in the soft light of the bedroom.

"You know Aunt Clare, I never thought much about him. He appeared and then he disappeared, but the one thing I do remember is being angry with him." Her face lit up with the lost memory of it all. "After Leora died, I felt angry with him. The day we went to spread her ashes I actually thought I saw a tear in his eye. Naturally, it surprised me because he had never mentioned her until I came to Oahu and after that had nothing to say to her. I saw the tear and I wondered why can't he ever show emotion? He shared with me then why he had shut me out, but it didn't matter anymore."

She uttered the words slowly, "I didn't care if he was my father, I didn't love him like I loved her and I never would. From that point on he and I coexisted in the house. He worked all the time and didn't even bother to say goodbye when I left for the airport to come here. Honestly, Aunt Clare I convinced myself that it didn't matter."

Aunt Clare nodded, "Why do you think you felt so much emotion tonight when you never had before?"

Cassie thought, "I think, well I think seeing him with a woman and never actually remembering him with my mother other than in pictures or in my imagination was a shock. That's all."

"Nothing else?" Aunt Clare asked.

"I guess it brought back all of the anger I felt after Leora died. You know Aunt Clare, it felt as if I had a door holding it all in and once I opened that door even a crack, I couldn't, actually I couldn't stop it. Everything came pouring out. Do you think I will feel like this forever?"

Aunt Clare laughed a little and said, "You found something very valuable tonight, something that a lot of us never learn. We think that if we shut our heart to someone that we will be able to open it up again, at will. That's not the case, and that's what you found out tonight. Even if you don't realize it consciously, my dear Cassandra, that's what you did. You shut your father and everyone else out when Leora died and tonight you let the door open. It is the holding it shut that is exhausting, not the letting it out."

She came over to the side of the bed, sat next to Cassie, put her arms around her, and held her. Finally, Cassie lay down, too exhausted to say anything more as Aunt Clare picked everything up and left the room, shutting the light off.

27

C assie's eyes flew open, squinted at the flowers on the yellow wallpaper, and recognized it as her bedroom in Maui. Why? She rubbed her eyes, sat up and looked out at the window recognizing the moon made everything in the room bright as the daytime. Everything remained in its rightful place, as she remembered it. The lone picture of her parents still in its frame, along with her books and drawing pens lined up on her desk. The door that led to the stairs wasn't open, which she thought strange. She opened it and carefully went down the stairs through a mist, smelling the distinctive sweet flowers of plumeria. All of the windows were open, but there were no trade winds, only the gentlest of breezes. As she approached the front door, it opened, inviting her into the night. She hoped no one would see her in her pajamas and then quickly dismissed it as silly because it was a dream.

She found the familiar banyan tree, arranged herself between its roots and waited. She had expected the ground to be wet, but instead its softness provided a gentle welcome, and the smell of its earthy minerals comforted her as she waited for the Menehune. *Surely, they would come* she thought as she closed her eyes. She felt her heart beating so strongly that she thought it might burst right out of her chest. At last she heard some rustling and surprisingly a voice, calling her.

"Cassie, oh Cassie girl. Come out and talk to me." She couldn't mistake that voice, the voice of Leora calling to her.

Quickly she stood and called, "Here I am Leora, here I am." In the darkness of the garden, she squinted and searched for a glimmer of light. Slowly, the familiar warm glow of the Menehune was all around her and the shape of the old Menehune woman became clearer, standing right in front of her, peering up at her curiously.

"Cassie, where are you? Where are you?" The voice of Leora originated from the Menehune woman.

Disappointment and then frustration caused tears to well up in Cassie's eyes. "But you're not her, where is she? Tell me where she is. I need to find her." The woman laughed and ran off back into the dark tangle of the garden vines. Cassie slumped to the ground and held her head in her hands. She felt no person come near and yet she heard a whisper: Leora's voice, whispering to her as if she were sitting right next to her. "Cassie my girl, to grow your love you must open your heart and move forward." Cassie tried to speak but no words came forth. She desperately wanted to see Leora, to be held and comforted by her. She lay down, sobbed on the banyan roots, and slept.

When next she opened her eyes, the sun reflecting off the lake filled the room. She panicked, fearing she had overslept and missed her meeting with her father and Hannah. She smelled coffee and bacon and the bedside clock reassured her that 7:00 a.m. gave her plenty of time to get ready. She dressed quickly, throwing on her good wool slacks, a pink sweater set, and her best pearls. As she searched for her coat, she saw something strange on the floor. Something green, the same green-gold of her dragon, Pinao Ula. She examined it, holding it up to the light and realized it was a wing, almost translucent with fine embedded webs. As she placed it in her palm to turn it over and get a better look, it disintegrated before her very eyes.

Then she remembered the dream, how she had waited for the Menehune under the banyan tree only to have them play a trick on her. Now this curious sign. She wanted to go back to find the Menehune and get some answers, to understand when exactly she had stopped feeling and closed the door on her emotions. She had heard the expression "to have a lump in your throat" but she hadn't understood what it meant. Now that she had experienced it, she didn't like it at all. Feelings apparently were difficult if not impossible to control, and that also frightened her. She wanted to ask the Menehune what all of this had to do with finding Pinao Ula's wing; did it mean The Gift had left her?

As she descended the staircase to the first floor, she looked out the large window to see the lake view and wondered what she would say to her father today. As she rounded the corner into the kitchen, she saw her aunt reading the Tribune as if nothing had happened. "Good morning Cassandra. Glad to see you up and about; if you hadn't appeared soon I planned to come and roust you out of bed. I saved some oatmeal and bacon, and Chef Joanie made some quiche that is still on top of the stove if you would like some. She's gone out shopping."

"Aunt Clare, I..." and she stood there feeling like an idiot. "I don't know how everything can change so much from day to day. I have to stop feeling this way."

"It's called emotion and why would you want to stop it?" Clare laughed.

"Yes, this emotion, how can I stop it?"

Again, Aunt Clare laughed and Cassie thought of Leora, which brought up another lump in her throat. She sighed and sat down in the large captain's chair, looked at her juice, and said, "I don't know if I can do this today, Aunt Clare. I don't know if I have the energy to be with them all day."

"Nonsense, you are a Bartholomew and you come from strong stock. You will go and will enjoy the time. Let's talk about where you should take them today." They spent the next hour planning the day's activities.

By the time Cassie walked out the door to get into the taxi for the short trip to the Drake she felt much better and had stopped feeling as if she might break into a flood of tears every five seconds. She reminded herself they would be gone soon.

As Cassie walked around the Chicago Art Museum that afternoon with her father and Hannah, she made her way up to the floors that housed religious art. With all of her newly awakened emotions, she had begun to think about the meaning of God and her own belief system. She had taken a course that semester called World Religions and became aware of her ignorance about religion of any kind. Because she had no formal religious upbringing, she didn't even know if her father had ever belonged to a church. She had no idea what he believed. She never prayed because she didn't know how. Looking at all of the pictures of Jesus and the Holy Family, Michael and his family came to her mind. What must it be like to grow up believing in something beyond this world, to know God and Jesus? Suddenly she felt small and ignorant because she never thought about questions such as what happens when we die or why we are here in the first place. She realized that throughout her entire life she had barely been there, only functioning on the surface and never even questioning such things.

She stood before an ancient piece. According to the little sign, the piece was a wooden portable altar, something the wealthy medieval family took with them wherever they went. Despite its age, it amazed her that the colors were still vibrant and the gold leaf still shone. The center panel depicted Mary holding the baby Jesus, who appeared to look straight at her, and it rather frightened her, so she moved on. Suddenly, everywhere and in every painting she saw the baby Jesus watching her and she wanted to know more about him.

She worked her way back downstairs to the Modern Art exhibit Hannah had wanted to see with its varied geometric shapes, dots and cartoonlike images that Cassie couldn't understand. She walked past a painting entitled, "The Lord Jesus praying in Gethsemane" and she stopped, touched by the vision of his pain and his suffering. She could see the emotion on his face although she didn't know much about the passion of

Christ. She did know that he had come to live, die, and rise again for her sins and her knowledge surprised her. Where had she heard that? It must have been when she had attended church with Michael. Curious how that had stuck with her all these months, she decided that she had had enough of baring her soul to these ancient paintings and she hurried on.

Before they went to the Aquarium, one of Cassie's favorite places, they suggested stopping for lunch and as they sat down for some of the famous Chicago pizza, she took note of her father. He actually looked more normal to her today, as he wore a shortsleeved plaid polo shirt and didn't slick his hair down as he typically did. Hannah looked like a model, dressed in peach tones with a finely knit cardigan that Cassie envied.

He smiled at her and took his hand in hers. "Cassie, what I didn't say last night was that we came here for a number of reasons, to Chicago, I mean," her father said. He seemed nervous and Cassie wondered now what major thing were they going to throw at her?

Hannah interjected, "Cassie, we have talked about many things already, but there's a few things we should discuss with you before the wedding. Actually, that's the first thing we should mention. We aren't going to have a big wedding. We are traveling to Europe, plan to be married there and then travel for a few weeks before returning to Honolulu. We wondered if it would upset you to not be present at the wedding."

"That's it?" Cassie shook her head; she got her thoughts together and made her speech. "I am glad you two found each other and last night, well, last night I realized that I have been living in a bubble all these years and I haven't, how can I say this, I haven't engaged in life? Father, I think you were doing the same thing. So if this is what you both want, please go ahead and know that I am thrilled for you. I hope you don't worry about me because I am excited to be out on my own and to start actually living instead of just being."

When she finished the most passionate speech either of them had heard from her they appeared a bit flabbergasted. "Bravo." Her father said. "Bravo, dear Cassie." He stood up to hug her, and with that, Cassie felt the lump in her throat return and she quickly sat and changed the subject. "Will you still keep the house or do you plan on moving?"

"No," Hannah looked at Andrew and shifted in her seat. "Let me explain. Your father has explained that the house you love is Leora's and that house is the one you would like to keep in the family. Isn't that so?"

"Absolutely correct," Cassie said with all of her former conviction returning.

"We understand, and we would like you to consider a proposition. Andrew and I propose selling the Manoa house and subdividing Leora's property so that we can build a house there. Of course Leora's main house and out buildings would all remain intact until you are ready to take ownership. Now please take a minute and think about it. We know that technically it is all your land at age 21, but would you be opposed to that idea in the meantime?"

As the plan sunk in, Cassie's eyes lit up and she smiled widely at them both. "I think that is a wonderful idea. I know what you said Father, that unless we sold off some of the property it would be a tax burden, but this seems to solve that problem. Plus, this way when I return someday and remodel the old house I will have neighbors."

Hannah looked relieved, took a rather large sip of her wine and smiled back. Visibly relieved, her father said, "Cassie, we are so glad to hear that you agree. We felt we should talk to you in person rather than over the phone. You know there are over 500 acres in all, more than we originally thought, and it requires a great deal of maintenance. When you have a break this summer we would like you to come home so we can talk about how to subdivide the property, and the arrangements. I would like to suggest that we lease the land from you so that you always own it and that Hannah will continue to occupy the house after I am gone, which is of course something we never like to think about." He smiled at his bride-to-be.

She sat there her mind awash with all of this news. She said aloud, "I think that is an excellent idea as well, there's a small field directly to the east of Leora's house that has a nice view, especially when the front palms are trimmed. You can almost see Diamond Head from there."

"Now that we are talking about the house we also have to repair the road going to the property. The last time I went up there the rain had all but washed it out," her father said.

"So exciting, isn't it Cassie?" Hannah clapped her hands and said, "Let's get on with our tour – we just can't sit here all day." As Cassie left them that evening for their romantic dinner for two, she thought to herself, I am no longer alone in this world. Today I gained both a father and a stepmother, I have Aunt Clare, and she thought warmly, I have Michael.

28

M rs. Martin answered the phone and said, "Cassie, I am so glad to hear your voice. We have missed you. You sound out of breath, are you feeling well?"

"I am Mrs. Martin, I am anxious to speak with Michael, is he home?"

"No, she said, "but he should be soon and I'll let him know that you called. Aren't you coming out for the weekend? It's the last weekend before school ends so we always plan a few special family events."

"We talked about it, Mrs. Martin, but we hadn't confirmed. That's one of the reasons I called." She hung up and went to get ready for dinner. *Wait until Aunt Clare hears all of my news, she'll fall off her chair,* she thought. That evening Cassie felt the best she had in a long time. After dinner, she and Aunt Clare went out on the balcony. To ward off the early spring chill coming off the lake, they brought heavy wool blankets and the two of them sat and watched the lights as they appeared on the lakefront. Cassie loved the transition from light until dark when the lake became a dark, foreboding expanse. She felt lightheaded and yes, she admitted to herself, she felt real happiness. She shared all the plans they had discussed that day and she saw that even Aunt Clare's eyes were teary in spite of her stoic self.

"Cassandra, tell me about this young man, Michael, is it serious?" Cassie put her mug down on the table in front of them, hugged her knees close to her, and wrapped the blanket even closer.

"Oh, Aunt Clare, I have never felt this way about anyone before. You see I didn't really date anyone in high school, but I had a very close friend named Zack. You may have heard Father mention him at dinner." Even as she said it, she felt a little twinge in her stomach. She had received another letter from him, but he hadn't mentioned anything about dating, only his classes and surfing. Cassie thought how strange that the two of them who barely spent a day apart since the fifth grade now didn't even keep in touch. She realized she hadn't answered her aunt. "I guess what I am trying to say is that I don't have much experience with dating, so feelings and dating, well this is all new to me. I love his family and even though he's attending graduate school at Notre Dame in the fall I hope we keep dating."

"Do you think it is wise to date exclusively at this point? As you point out, you haven't had much experience with the opposite sex."

Cassie laughed, "No, you're right there, Aunt Clare I haven't. It will be a busy summer with going home, seeing Leora's house and my friend Zack. I think I'll be okay; anyway, the truth is I haven't really met anyone else I would be interested in dating anyway." She thought that it would be important to spend time with Zack. Now that her heart and head were open, maybe there were feelings there that needed exploring. She also hoped that this weekend she and Michael might talk about the future.

The weekend ended in disaster. At first, everything seemed fine, she enjoyed pizza, and card games with the entire Martin clan. Later in the evening, she and Michael took a walk and she noticed something different about him, he seemed far away and not as focused on her as usual. She finally took his hand, shook it and said, "Hey are you in there? What's going on?"

As they rounded the corner back to his house, he said, "Cassie, I think we need to talk. Let's go into the back porch." The back screen porch ran the entire length of the house. They walked around to the back yard to enter the porch and settled onto the large wicker couch. Michael turned to face Cassie. She already felt a sinking feeling that went from her stomach down to her feet. She had been so excited to see him tonight, to share with him everything that had happened and now something felt terribly wrong. She didn't think she wanted to hear what he had to say.

"Cassie, listen to me. You know how I feel about you. I have made it very clear that you are different from anyone I have ever been with and that I care about you, right?" She nodded, now more afraid than ever. "Well, it's like this."

Now he couldn't look her in the eye, but stood up and began pacing around the porch. "You remember I told you about the girl I dated all through high school, right?" She nodded and folded her hands in her lap gripping them tightly to control herself. "It turns out, she is coming home for the summer and we have been talking and well, she thinks, I mean, I think maybe we should give our relationship another chance."

Cassie listened intently for more and as she heard the words, she had difficulty believing that he was telling her he wanted to get back together with his high-school sweetheart. She stood up, trying not to let out the emotion she had only recently discovered and said as stoically as she could, "Michael, there's nothing more to say then. Please take me back to Aunt Clare's. I'll go and get my bag. There's no point in staying here."

He tried to touch her arm, but looked as if he would cry so she quickly pulled away and ran up the stairs to Mitzi's room and shut the door, thankful that the rest of the family was in the basement playing a loud game of ping-pong.

One little sob escaped, but she swallowed it, determined not to let him see her cry, and ran back down the stairs to where he waited at the front door. She thought, *let him tell his family what happened, I can't face them.*

Silence filled the car on the drive back. Michael tried twice to say something, but he stopped himself. They had made plans for the following Friday night, but she decided not to mention it and neither did he. It took every part of her being to control herself and not break down and as a result, her entire body began to shake violently.

Finally, they pulled up in front of the large building on Lake Shore Drive. Cassie jumped out, grabbed her bag from the back seat, and went into the front entrance, proud that she never looked back at him even after he called her name. Thankfully, she had her own key, as she knew that Aunt Clare would still be at the opera. She quickly penned a note at the front entrance table so that she would see it when she came in and ran up to her bedroom, grateful to be alone. She could now allow herself to feel the full extent of his words. As she lay in the dark, she felt anger, disappointment, and sadness. In the end, when she thought about how he played with her emotions, she felt more anger than anything. The first boy she had ever really liked and all because he convinced her that he found her special. She had to admit that a spark of chemistry happened when they were together, no denying that. When she thought of the embarrassment of telling Aunt Clare, after she had been so sure that they would be dating in the fall, it led to the inevitable lump in her throat, and the tears returned. Sobbing and lying face down on the sheets, she could smell the rosewater rinse that Aunt Clare used throughout the house. While she usually found it comforting, now she felt nauseated and began sobbing so hard that suddenly she began gasping for air. She couldn't breathe, and chest pains began, sharper and more crushing than ever before. She tried to sit up and panicked, not knowing what to do to stop the pain. She slowly made her way to the bathroom and found the medication in the bag Dr. Martin had given her in the event of chest pains. She glanced in the mirror and while the crushing pain had subsided a bit, she saw that her face was white, completely devoid of color. She took the pill and made her way to the bed, taking a cold cloth with her. She turned the lights on and opened the door hoping that her Aunt would see it as an invitation to stop in when she arrived home.

When Aunt Clare saw Cassie's note she immediately knew something terrible had happened. As she entered the room, what she saw alarmed her. Cassie lay on top of the bed, her face chalky white, eyes closed and not moving. "Cassandra, wake up, wake up." At first, Cassie didn't respond but finally she opened her eyes.

Clare shook her lightly, "What in God's name happened?" Cassie told her briefly what happened and how she thought her heart would explode, but she took the medicine and felt better now. Aunt Clare helped Cassie into her pajamas and then into bed. She whispered, "Cassandra, I know you feel as if your heart has been broken, but trust me. You will recover and life will go on." But she could see that Cassie had already fallen asleep.

Once more Cassie smelled the garden before she even opened her eyes. As she did she felt a twinge of excitement, that this time she would find the Menehune and demand some answers. This didn't look like her garden, she thought as she stood up and began to see through the dim haze that surrounded her. She saw him, a Menehune larger than most, almost three feet tall walking away from her. She quickly followed, but not being able to reach him, she called out, at the same time knowing he might easily disappear. "Please, stop, please." She begged him to stop but he only moved faster, almost running through the dark forest. She couldn't catch him. She put everything she had into it, running faster than she ever had until finally she reached out and caught him by his white shirt and he turned. The Menehune's face was Zack's face. She fainted.

Cassie appeared at the breakfast table as if it were a normal morning. They had the final appointment with the last specialist that morning and then she would return to her dorm. She felt as though her legs were made of lead and she wanted to vomit when she smelled the eggs and bacon in front of her. Aunt Clare came in just as the maid started to take her plate away.

"Cassandra Leora Bartholomew. You are not going to start this. Leave her plate please, and bring me a cup of strong tea. Thank you." As the maid left the room, Cassie looked up at Aunt Clare, her eyes brimming with tears. "Now Cassandra, you listen to me. We have a great deal to do today and you need to get back to school. There's barely six weeks left before you return home. I understand that you haven't experienced much emotion your entire life, but you are making up for lost time now. I also know that it hurts as much as any physical pain and you want it to stop, but it is part of life and you must pick yourself up and carry on."

Cassie nodded, began to eat her breakfast, and found it rather cold. She picked at the bacon and started to say something but the words were stuck. Finally she spoke. "Of course, Aunt Clare, I know that's what I need to do, but it came as such a shock to me, that's all. Here I kept thinking about how much fun we had this year and even though he would be at

Notre Dame…." Her voice trailed off as she stared at her plate again.

"Cassandra, look at me." She waited for her to look up. "Your grandmother and your mother were very strong women and I know you are too. You simply got off on the wrong foot emotionally when you lost your mother and they sent you away by yourself. Trust me when I say this. You didn't have a normal childhood, but you are having a normal young adulthood. I tried to warn you the other night about getting too serious without any experience. Bartholomews are strong people who continue to move forward even when things don't go our way, and we never, ever, wallow in self-pity."

Cassie listened, as she had never heard her aunt speak so sharply and with such conviction about anything personal. Aunt Clare had strong opinions about Chicago politics, and of the state of the world, but she had never had this kind of a conversation with Cassie. It had the desired effect. Cassie sat up straighter in her chair and began to eat. She looked at her aunt with new appreciation. "Aunt Clare, thank you. I know that I should move on and I will. Now that this has happened, I suddenly realize that I am looking forward to going home for the summer. I need to see my friend Zack. He and I haven't been very good at writing each other letters and I want to find out why."

Aunt Clare sighed a loud sigh of relief. "Now that's the spirit of our family, Cassie girl." Cassie was shocked because not once this past year had she called her by her nickname. It sounded like music to her ears.

She got up from her chair, came around to the other side of the table, and hugged her aunt around the neck. "Oh Aunt Clare, you are the best. I still feel sick inside, but at least my outside is back to normal." She decided that before they left for the doctor's office she would write Zack and make sure he knew she wanted to see him the minute she landed on Oahu.

29

S he received a telegram and some postcards from her Father and Hannah on their honeymoon trip to Europe. They would return to Hawaii two days before she did and promised to send a driver to pick her up.

She had done well in her final exams and had almost finished packing when Mitzi appeared in her doorway. Mary Ann, her roommate, had already checked out and said goodbye with a sincere promise to write over the summer.

"Hey you." Mitzi came around the corner smiling at her. "I missed seeing you the last few weeks. Michael told us what happened."

"He did? What did he tell you?"

"Just that the love of his life has come to her senses and they're back together. He wouldn't say anything about how you took the news. Cassie, I have to tell you the whole family is sick about this and we miss you terribly."

"Mitzi, sit down. I have to share something with you. I have learned something very important during these past few weeks. As much as I liked Michael, what I liked more was being part of a real family like the one you have. I never had that, Mitzi, and it felt so good to know what that feels like, to belong. If I ever do find someone that I love enough to marry, I want to have a family life with as much joy as yours." With tears running down her cheeks, she reached out and hugged Mitzi with all her strength. She had come to realize that for most of her life she hadn't experienced another human being's touch. Michael's kisses and bear hugs made her aware of how devoid her entire life had been of human contact. The combination of all of this emotion and physical contact made her even more anxious to get home and see Zack. She felt a sense of urgency about it, although she couldn't explain it. She spent a few days at Aunt Clare's before the driver took her to O'Hare and although Michael had called once to check in, she asked Aunt Clare to make an excuse, because she really didn't want to talk to him. Her dreams had become repetitive, every night the same dream. She would awake in her garden, under her banyan tree, but the Menehune wouldn't come to her. When she did see them off in the forest they would laugh, wave at her and run away. She concluded that they were saying goodbye.

On the plane home to Honolulu, her mind felt jumbled with thoughts and feelings. It was a good thing the flight took a long time because she felt as if she needed every minute to think. Father and Hannah had recently returned home and now focused on selling the house and designing their new home. Try as she might she didn't feel sad to see them sell the old house in Manoa, although at one time it felt like home to her. As the plane landed her legs started feeling a little shaky. But she didn't know why.

Even without seeing the landscape, she knew immediately she had returned to the island. Her arms had always been cold in Chicago and here the tropical breeze, unlike the cool lake breezes off Lake Michigan, felt like a sweet caress to her. She collected her baggage and slowly made her way out of the familiar airport to where the driver always met her. She didn't see the driver or the car. She saw a number of people waiting for passengers to emerge and there stood one muscular young man, obviously a surfer. He waved to her and she hurried toward him. He ran over to her and she instinctively hugged him. "Oh, Zack, no one told me you would be here."

"I know, I called your father and told him he better not let a driver pick you up, I wanted that privilege." Now he lifted her, hugged her, and swung her around at the same time. She couldn't stop smiling and staring at him.

"Zack, now about the letter-writing thing" she began as he loaded her bags into the trunk.

"Cass, please don't say a word. Let's both agree that we are the world's worst letter writers." As he slammed the trunk he turned to her and hugged her hard, pulling her up off the ground at the same time – and then he kissed her. He really kissed her and this time it felt as if no one had kissed her before. This is home, she thought, this is where I belong, why didn't I see it before? Someone honked their horn, and the police officer in charge gave Zack the move on signal and they both jumped in the car.

Cassie felt the oddest feeling inside. She thought of the Pinao Ula, and then she realized that the excitement of seeing Zack and the anticipation at what would happen next reminded her of when she first thought she had swallowed the Pinao Ula.

They agreed that in spite of it being her first night back she would tell her father that she wanted to have dinner with Zack. She would promise to go to Leora's the next day with them, so she hoped they wouldn't mind. As Zack took her suitcases up to the porch, she looked around. It didn't look much different, although there were a lot more white flowers in the yard than last year. She wondered if Hannah had something to do with the new landscaping, as her father never had any interest in it.

They came outside as soon as they heard them pull up to the house. Her father looked younger than the last time she saw him, but Hannah struck her as even more breathtaking in a tropical white outfit adorned with a red necklace, earrings and bracelet. She tried to introduce Zack, but Hannah waved a hand at her. "Cassie, not necessary, I met Zack a while back and now we are very good friends." She laughed and Zack shrugged as if to say, what do you expect me to say?

After Zack drove off, she entered the house with them, expecting to hear about their trip until it would be time for Zack to pick her up. She knew that although she wanted to take a nap in order to get back on island time she mustn't sleep until evening. Her father and Hannah were even more animated than they were that last day in Chicago and she could see how happy they were together. Architectural drawings, fabric swatches and pictures of furniture covered the entire dining-room table. It painted a clear picture of their dream home.

She needed a few minutes to herself to think things through and prepare to meet with Zack. She felt as though her emotions were delicate, as if the roller coaster she had been on lately would continue. On the other hand, she thought proudly, I am getting used to this roller coaster of emotions and maybe enjoying it just a little.

As she and Zack drove out to Leora's after dinner at a favorite place in Manoa, she could feel herself becoming more and more anxious about the prospect of being alone with him. They had talked about everything, as usual, over dinner. He had shared his experiences dating and she shared the facts about Michael, and it seemed as though no time had passed since she had left for Chicago. Her excitement grew as they drove up the familiar road and she could see the house. Her father had kept the property maintained, because no overgrowth interfered with her view of the setting sun.

She opened the door, Zack behind her with a small cooler of drinks to enjoy the sunset. They worked quickly, taking the protective sheets off the chairs and placing them into position to see the sun set over the water. Zack opened two wine coolers and they settled in, both quiet for a long moment.

As dusk approached Cassie spoke, "Zack, let me say something. I have so much to tell you I don't know where to start." Their chairs were close and his arm touched hers.

He looked at her and he laughed. "Cassie, some things never change. Don't you know that you are the most wonderful girl and that I have missed you?" He stood up and pulled her to her feet. "Let's start over."

he said and he kissed her as hard as she had ever been kissed while he held her tightly. Finally, he stopped kissing her, but wouldn't release her.

"Cassie, nothing else matters except that you are here and we are together again. I learned that over the past year. I don't care about anything else." At that point, Cassie didn't need to read his thoughts, she knew he loved her and she loved him. She had reconnected with her soulmate and words were unnecessary.

Cassie remembered her mother's words that she had memorized long ago, that things aren't always what they appear to be. She knew now that she didn't love Michael, but she had loved Zack all along. She had learned that her father loved her even when he didn't show it.

Zack had spoken the truth; there was no need to say anything else. As they lay on the ground looking up at the stars, she felt secure in his arms and knew that the future would bring only happiness.

"Zack, did I ever tell you I could read minds?"

"Well, tell me what I am thinking now," he whispered as he took her in his arms and kissed her again.